I never tho...

Levi's words cut through Zoe like a hot poker.

Maybe she was a coward. Afraid to leave the building. Afraid to share her secret with anyone close to her—afraid to let anyone get too close. Afraid to seize the love she'd so briefly found with a patient, protective, rugged Marine this past summer.

Afraid, afraid, afraid.

Her life had taken some dramatic turns over the last few months, and she wasn't coping well. She didn't want the rest of the world to know about the baby before she told Levi.

And she certainly didn't want *him* to know.

How to Hurt Zoe.

She had the words from the very first letter memorized. They'd been a textbook example of how a stalker could isolate her and drive everything that mattered from her life.

She cupped her hand around her lower belly where she felt flutters of movement. But not this. Never this. *He* would never get his hands on her baby.

CRIME SCENE K-9

JULIE MILLER

Harlequin

INTRIGUE

Moms Group. Dear, longtime friends who read my books and know stuff. ;)

Thanks for brainstorming some plot points with me over our yummy, gossipy monthly lunches.

Harlequin®
INTRIGUE™

Recycling programs for this product may not exist in your area.

ISBN-13: 978-1-335-69008-1

Crime Scene K-9

Copyright © 2025 by Julie Miller

Harlequin Enterprises ULC
22 Adelaide St. West, 41st Floor
Toronto, Ontario M5H 4E3, Canada
www.Harlequin.com

Printed in Lithuania

MIX
Paper | Supporting responsible forestry
FSC® C021394

Julie Miller is an award-winning *USA TODAY* bestselling author of breathtaking romantic suspense—with a National Readers' Choice Award and a Daphne du Maurier Award, among other prizes. She has also earned an *RT Book Reviews* Career Achievement Award. For a complete list of her books, monthly newsletter and more, go to juliemiller.org.

Books by Julie Miller

Harlequin Intrigue

Protectors at K-9 Ranch

Shadow Survivors
K-9 Defender
Special Forces K-9
Protecting the Pack
Crime Scene K-9

Kansas City Crime Lab

K-9 Patrol
Decoding the Truth
The Evidence Next Door
Sharp Evidence

The Taylor Clan: Firehouse 13

Crime Scene Cover-Up
Dead Man District

Visit the Author Profile page at Harlequin.com.

CAST OF CHARACTERS

Master Sergeant Levi Callahan—A week of comfort, passion and, he thought, love kept the Marine going as he finished his last deployment. But when Zoe ghosts him, he's hurt. Then angry. When he gets home to Kansas City, this military cop tracks her down and demands answers. He's not prepared for the secret that awaits him...or the danger.

Zoe Stockman—Criminalist at the KCPD Crime Lab. Her anxiety disorder once made her easy pickings for a serial killer. She escaped his clutches, but now someone is using the same psych games to torment her. There's a cruel copycat in her world, and the only one she can turn to for protection is the one man who wants nothing to do with her. Can she convince Levi to be her champion—for his unborn baby?

Sky—Levi's K-9 partner. In his doggy heart, he'll always be a Marine.

Gus Packard and Poppy Hunter—Zoe's neighbors.

Ethan Wynn—He's serving three life sentences for murder.

Arlo Wynn—Ethan's cousin.

Jordan Fletcher—A reporter.

Emily Hartman—Zoe is investigating her disappearance.

Chapter One

24 July...

Master Sergeant Levi Callahan booted up the computer in the communications building and reached down to pet a panting Sky, his German shepherd partner, who stretched out across his sandy boots beneath the table while he waited for the program to come up.

"Hurry up and wait," he groaned. He breathed deeply, fighting to slow his elevated heart rate and rapid breathing after that sprint across the base from the front gate. Summer in the Middle East was no joke. Even at ten in the morning, it was a hundred degrees. So, the air-conditioning needed to keep the computers and communications equipment cool was a welcome respite.

But spending time out of the sun and sand and heat wasn't why he and Sky had run.

Even a month ago, he wouldn't have been this eager to grab the earliest slot available for communicating with the home front back in the States. Sure, he had a sister and a best friend, who was now married to said sister, to call and catch up with. But Lexi and Aiden understood the demands of his career as a military cop and dog handler in the Corps, and they didn't mind when he had to cancel a call home or even not respond to an email for several days. They'd worry, sure, if his priorities changed and he had to delay messaging home—but they understood.

He wasn't calling home this morning. Time and timing were precious to him now. Because something had changed the week he'd been home on leave over the Fourth of July holiday.

He'd met Zoe Stockman.

Zoe who'd had a panic attack at the large gathering of friends and coworkers celebrating Independence Day. Zoe who'd let the big ol' Marine who'd noticed her white-knuckled grip on the arms of her lawn chair comfort her. Zoe who'd let her boss's big brother hold her hand, then hold her in his lap, then get her out of there when it all got to be too much.

Levi had spent most of the next several days with Zoe. Most of the nights, too.

He'd fallen in love.

At the age of thirty-eight, when he'd been considering the possibilities of bachelorhood or settling for a woman who'd make a good partner, Levi had been blindsided by the blue-eyed beauty. Way smarter than he'd ever be, quiet, vulnerable, Zoe had needed him in a way that spoke to his desire to be of service to others and his loyalty to a team, to the Corps and to his country.

She listened, too. That first night had been all about holding her and helping her sleep and recharge for a new day. But then they'd driven down to Truman Lake where they'd gone for a long walk, and they'd talked. They'd done some touristy things. He'd met her for lunch. He visited the Kansas City Crime Lab, where she worked as a criminalist.

They'd talked about his service, why he'd enlisted after high school. They'd discussed his parents' tragic deaths and her mother's passing from cancer. They discovered a shared love for dogs, snow, Italian food and Royals baseball. They'd discussed her anxiety issues and how she was treating her condition with therapy, lifestyle changes and occasional medication. They'd strategized what he might do with his life when his stint in the Corps was up in December—what types of jobs he'd be suited for, if he'd need further education, what his second career might be.

And they'd kissed. They'd made out. His last night before catching his flight out of KCI Airport, they'd made love. He hadn't intended to take things that far. But when he'd told her he was worried about how fragile she was and didn't want to make anything worse, Zoe had gotten pissed. Then she'd proceeded to show him just how remarkably strong she was once she got out of her head and focused on achieving the thing she wanted. That first time had been a wild battle of wills that'd had him so out of his mind with lust that he'd barely gotten a condom on. He'd held her tightly in his arms afterward. And just before dawn, after a couple hours of sleep, he'd made love to her with all the tenderness and emotion that filled his heart.

Then they'd checked in with his sister, brother-in-law and his K-9 partner, and his niece one last time before racing to the airport. They'd exchanged phone numbers, emails, addresses and promises to keep in touch as often as they could before he mustered out near the end of the year and returned to Kansas City. They'd kissed, she'd smiled and then he had to walk away.

Something inside Levi had changed irrevocably that last night. He'd found the purpose, the person he could devote the next twenty years of his life to—and hopefully, far beyond that. Zoe wasn't a shore-leave conquest or even a friends-with-benefits partner. She was it. For him, at any rate.

So yeah, he was antsy about making this long-distance connection with her after two weeks apart.

Picking up on the tension that must've been radiating off him, Sky whined and crawled out from beneath the table and wedged his long, black muzzle beneath Levi's arm, resting his head in Levi's lap.

"Good boy." He scratched around the shepherd's ears and smoothed his hand along the dog's back and patted his flanks to ease his whining while they waited for the satellite feeds to connect. Levi and Sky were as in tune with each other as he'd ever been with a human partner. And Sky was always willing to take the extra step to make sure Levi was all right. "Yeah, buddy, I am nervous. She's kind of quiet and not always sure of herself, but I think you'll like her. She's sweet and compassionate. And if she feels safe, she'll show you she has a temper, too." Sky tilted his dark head from one side to the other, listening to the tone of Levi's words if not actually understanding them. "She'll probably try to spoil you. You're going to meet her one of these days. I promise."

This was the first time in a lot of years that Levi could see the next phase of his life. When he retired from the Corps, Sky would retire with him. His plans had been as nebulous as *I'm moving home to Kansas City, and I'll find a place to live that takes dogs.* But now, thanks to the woman on the other end of this call, he wasn't just going home because that was what he knew from his past as a civilian—he was moving toward something. He was moving toward a future with the beautiful woman who had captured his heart in the span of one short week.

Zoe Stockman. His future.

"Pick up, Zo." His foot was tapping again. "Come on, pick up."

The call went through with a soft beep, and he grinned from ear to ear, waiting for Zoe to click the button at her end. His screen filled with a swirl of colors and shadows, and he realized she was too close to the camera on her laptop for him to make out any details. "Zoe?"

He heard a breathy sigh and a grumble about falling asleep in her makeup. And then the swirls of color took form as Zoe sat back against her gray sofa with a trio of fuchsia, bubblegum and baby-pink pillows behind her and a fuzzy blanket pulled up over her lap where it blended in with her pink Kansas City Chiefs T-shirt. Yep, pink was her signature color. She even drove a rose-colored SUV that she'd dubbed Pinky. She was a woman of fascinating contrasts—a true tomboy raised with brothers by a widowed father, with a love for science and sports. Yet she was a girly-girl when it came to her design choices and the way she could rock a little black dress.

She pushed a long strand of hair off her cheek and tucked it behind her ear. "Hey, Levi. Have you been trying to reach me? I'm sorry. I dozed off."

Man, she was pretty. The woman had a serious case of bedhead, and she was still freakin' adorable. Dark hair swept up on top of her head in a bun that had been tugged to one side, with wavy strands tumbling over one cheek and smooshed up beside her ear on the other. She had clear, pale skin, lips tinted with a smear of orchid-pink lip gloss, and big blue eyes with a smudge of mascara above the apple of her cheek. She had a crease from the smudge down to her chin that matched the trim on the pillows behind her.

"*Rumpled with sleep* is a good look on you," he teased.

Although she smiled at the compliment, she rolled her eyes and shook her head. "I was all dolled up for you an hour ago." Her gaze dropped to her own image at the bottom corner of her screen, and her eyes widened. Things stirred behind the zipper of his utility cammies when she poked her thumb into her mouth and sucked on the tip before using it to wipe away the smeared mascara. "You should have warned me that I looked like a clown."

How the woman could look so innocent yet be so sexy at the same time was a mystery he was willing to spend the rest of his life trying to solve. "All I see is a beautiful woman whose jerk boyfriend woke her up in the middle of the night."

"You're not a jerk," she quickly argued. "I knew with the

time difference this call was going to be late." She plucked at the blanket, a subtle sign he'd learned meant that nerves were setting in. "I… I wasn't sure you were still going to call. Or maybe that I had the wrong night."

Uh-uh. She wasn't going to put any blame for a miscommunication on herself. "You had the time right. I'm the one who's late. I got held up with work."

The fiddling with the blanket stopped as she turned her focus toward him again. "Something dangerous?"

"It turned out not to be. But Sky and I had to make sure. We're responsible for the security of over eight thousand Marines, sailors and civilian personnel on this base. I don't take that job lightly."

"They're lucky to have you and your team watching over them." Her eyes darted back and forth, searching the screen. "Is Sky with you?"

"Right here." Good. He wanted to talk about her, *them* this morning, not his job and the dangers and frustrations he faced on a daily basis. He had buddies in the barracks or at Mess he could talk shop with. But there was only one woman he could talk to about feelings, fun and a future.

Levi tapped his chest. "Sky, up." The dog rose and braced his front paws against Levi's chest, eagerly anticipating the reward of petting and praise he was sure to get for obeying. "That's my man. Good boy. Good Sky." Once he had the dog framed in the picture, he issued another command. "Sky, right."

On cue, Sky turned his muzzle to the right, leaving a nose print on the computer screen. Levi immediately pulled back and wiped away the mark with the side of his fist. "Oops. Better get rid of that. Hard to explain the smear to the next user."

Zoe's laughter and voice kept the dog's attention pointed toward the screen. "Hi, big guy. You're a handsome boy." Zoe smiled at the dog before tilting her gaze back up to Levi's. "I'm impressed. He did everything you asked him to do."

"We work on his training every day. It keeps those skills fresh, but it's also a bonding time between the two of us. We work as one unit most of the time."

She sighed heavily. "I miss having a dog. We always had them at home growing up. Duke was my sweetheart. Terrible hunting dog according to Dad, but a great pet. He got me through my teenage angst."

He suspected a well-trained dog would be a good thing for Zoe as an adult, too, to alert her to panic attacks so she could get someplace where she could safely shut down or simply to have someone to distract her or cuddle with when her anxiety did get the best of her. "He's eager to meet you."

There was a sharp rap at the door behind him. Sky swung around and gave a warning bark that made Levi's ears ring in the tiny room. "Easy, boy. He's one of us."

The door opened and the corporal who'd shown him in held up five fingers. "You've got five minutes, Top."

"Oorah, Delacorte." The door closed, and Sky settled his top half back across Levi's lap as Zoe started talking again.

"That's a scary bark," she observed. "You taking care of your daddy, Sky?"

Despite his partner's interest in the lady saying his name, Levi pushed the dog down to lie on the floor beside him. "We're more like bros than me being his daddy. But yeah, we've got each other's backs."

Zoe smiled, and the darkness inside him lightened at the simple gesture. "I'm glad you're so careful."

"When I can be." Levi checked his own watch and frowned. "We're down to a less than five-minute window. Since I can't say too much about my job, what are you up to?"

They talked a little about her current assignment at the crime lab. "I've been working a missing-person case…signs of a struggle, potential kidnapping from the place the victim was last seen. Although, according to the detectives, there hasn't been any ransom demand. I don't mind days in the lab, processing evidence. But I really prefer working the actual crime scene. Even when it's scary, like a woman in danger. That's where I feel like I can help the most."

Levi swallowed down his own trepidation that *she* could be the woman in danger when she was at a crime scene. "That's because you're so good at it. My sister says so. She told me that you're in your element finding clues."

"I guess so. It's all those Nancy Drew and Agatha Christie mysteries I read growing up." She started plucking at the blanket in her lap again, and Levi wondered what was making her nervous. "Unless there's a big crowd of onlookers. Or the media's there. There was a reporter at that crime scene who wanted to interview me. He wants to do a whole series of articles on me. Sort of a day-in-the-life of a criminalist— following me from the crime scene to the verdict at the end of a trial and what my role would be in all of that. He said I was the most photogenic science geek he'd seen at a crime scene." Levi watched her shiver at the thought and wished he was there to hold her hand or put his arms around her. "I told him no. I don't like the spotlight."

"He was out of line," the military cop in him commented, not liking the idea of the reporter zeroing in on Zoe because of her looks. Or singling her out, period, while she was doing her job. "Good for you for knowing yourself and saying what you needed to."

"I guess. I referred him to Lexi. But I got the idea he didn't want to talk to my supervisor."

Levi frowned as her hands fisted around the edge of the blanket. "I can tell his request upset you. You taking care of yourself?"

"Doing my best. I'm practicing those mental exercises my

therapist gave me. And, thanks to your advice, I now belong to a gym. I run on their track, and I started a yoga class. I still like long walks the best, though, when it comes to exercise." She sighed heavily and loosened her grip on the blanket. He couldn't help but remember the night she'd held on to him so tightly, and missed how her needy touch had made him feel like he was her anchor in her storm of emotions. "You were right. Your suggestion about getting regular exercise and getting my BDNFs pumping has been helpful."

"What are BDNFs?"

"Brain-derived neurotrophic factors," she explained, as if those were words normal people used every day. "It's a protein molecule in our brains that promotes the growth of new brain cells. Which, in turn, improves our memory, learning and coping abilities."

Made sense once she'd explained it, even to a guy like him who had more life experience than time in a classroom. "Man, I love it when you get all smarticle on me."

"Smarticle?"

"It's my own word. With two college degrees and a brain that won't quit, you're loaded with smarticles, which I find extremely attractive."

She giggled, then rested her elbow on her knee and her chin in her hand. "Most guys would call me a nerd or a head case or just stare at me with a stupefied look on their face when I give an explanation like that. You make me smile, Levi Callahan."

"Good. Then my mission has been a success." He liked being the guy who could make her feel better. But he wasn't thrilled to hear that others hadn't been so patient with her specific needs. "But if I ever hear anybody calling you a head case, I'm taking him out at the knees or siccing Sky on him."

Both Zoe and Sky sat up at the tension in his tone. Levi put his hand on the dog's head to reassure him that nothing was amiss, and the longing look Zoe gave him reassured Levi that he hadn't upset her.

"You make me feel safe, too. I... I haven't felt that secure about the world around me for a long time. Until you were there." Then, as if she had revealed too much, she shrugged and took a drink from the water bottle beside her. "Just an FYI—no matter how much exercise, BDNFs and endorphins help me, I will never get up at five a.m. to work out the way you do."

He let her change the subject. "Hey, after twenty years of the military making me do it, it's become a habit. Gives me a reason to get up and get my day started." He'd either have to keep up the fitness routine or find other meaningful motivators to get him going in the morning once he retired to civilian life. "But I look forward to taking some of those long walks with you."

"I do, too. I miss you. I liked seeing you every day."

"Me, too." He did already have one part of his plan in mind for life outside of the Marine Corps. "We'll make up for lost time. It'll be just the two of us. We'll spend as much time as we can together, really get to know each other."

"The two of us," she echoed. Then her face squinched up in an adorable frown. "We're not moving too fast, are we? I mean, we only had a week, and now we're so far apart—"

"That's why we're making the effort to stay in touch. We'll make up for lost time when we're together again. I see you and me as a long-term thing, Zo," he confessed. "I want you to get comfortable enough with me that you see us the same way."

"I think I want that, too."

"I'll be as patient as I need to be until you *know* you want that, too."

A knock on the door warned him that the next Marine was here to claim his or her call time. Sky woofed—more of an *I'm aware you're there* announcement rather than any actual alarm—at the corporal who stuck his head in the door. "Need to wrap it up, Top."

"Easy, boy." Levi patted Sky's muscular flank, praising him for his almost preternatural awareness of their surroundings. "I'm sorry, babe, but I need to go. The next guy on the list is waiting for his turn."

Zoe scooted forward, a curious expression on her face. "Why does that man call you Top?"

"It's a nickname for my rank—Master Sergeant. I'm a top-level NCO."

"Noncommissioned officer?"

"That's right."

She smiled, looking pleased that he'd confirmed her information. "I'm reading a book on military-speak. I want to understand everything you say when we talk."

"You don't have to do that."

"I'm investing in this relationship, too, Levi. If I'm spouting science and you don't understand, I want you to tell me. And if you're being all Master Sergeant or primo dog trainer on me, I want to understand you, too."

Yeah. Zoe Stockman was the woman he wanted. He was important to her. She cared about him. She needed him. She made him feel all the things that tragically becoming a parent and breadwinner at the age of eighteen had stolen from him. Not that he regretted one second the decisions he'd made to support his sister, Lexi. He was proud to serve his country and protect his fellow servicemen and -women. He loved the discipline, the action. He loved working with Sky, solving crimes and saving lives.

But twenty years of taking and giving orders, of doing the right thing, the responsible thing—even if it was the hard thing—had robbed him of the chance to find out who he was outside of the Corps. Zoe made him feel like a younger man inside—not the ranking old man his years of service had demanded of him. She made him feel like he could be something different, something more than Master Sergeant Callahan. A husband, maybe. A father when the time was right. He had a feeling that Zoe might be his reward for all his years of service and sacrifice. "You're sweet, Zo. I wish we had more time tonight."

Her cheeks colored with a delightful blush. "I won't keep you any longer. Besides, I've been exhausted lately. If I don't get eight hours of sleep, then I have to take a nap after work. Like an old woman."

Levi leaned forward, too. "You feeling okay? You said your meds made you drowsy."

"I haven't had to take anything since you were here. No big panic attacks. I mean, I wasn't a fan of that reporter pestering me, but Aiden and Blue were there, and they chased him away before I wigged out on anyone." Knowing Levi's brother-in-law, a KCPD cop, and his K-9 partner were keeping an eye on Zoe lessened his concern. "Work keeps my brain engaged. Exercise keeps my body in tune." She rubbed her hand across her belly and grimaced. "I don't know. Maybe I've got a touch of the summer flu."

"Take care of yourself. Fluids and rest, according to my sister and the medics here on base."

"Sounds like good advice. You keep your head down and be safe, too." Another knock on the door and the monitor stepped in and tapped his watch. "Looks like you have to go."

"Yeah. I lo…" It was way too early in their relationship to say those three little words. "Let's do this again soon. Chats, emails, calls—whatever and whenever we can make it happen. Send letters if we have to. Lord knows I haven't gotten anything at mail call lately. You're the highlight of my week, Zo."

"Same here. Pet Sky for me, and take care of yourself."

"You, too. By the end of December, we'll be doing this in person."

"I can't wait to feel your arms around me again."

"Nothing has ever felt as good as holding you." Levi put his hand on the screen, wishing he could feel silky hair and warm skin instead of hard plastic. But Zoe lifted her hand to her screen, too, and their fingers touched across time and distance. Something in him settled. "Bye, Zo."

"Bye, Le…" The screen went dark, and she was gone.

THE FIGURE SITTING in the shadows studied the array of photographs spread out on the table. Nostrils flared. A pulse raced.

The images were all of the same woman—from various distances, in different settings, taken at different times of day or night.

One beautiful, blissfully unaware woman.

Yes, she'd do very nicely. This was the way in, the big break that would get a person noticed, help them stand out from the crowd. This woman could change everything.

With this target and this plan, a happily-ever-after would be guaranteed. That was really all anyone could want.

And the woman in the pictures would never see it coming.

The photographer smiled and went to work.

Chapter Two

1 September...

Levi sat in his bunk and listened to Zoe apologize over the phone. Again.

This was the third time she'd cancelled a face-to-face chat on the computer and had opted to call him on his cell. "Sorry I haven't been able to do a FaceTime chat. I've been working a lot of nights, and the hours are just too crazy to schedule something like that. Either we're getting summoned out on a call or..."

"Or what?"

Her hesitation made him think she was buying time to come up with something. "I... I'm just not comfortable making a long personal call while I'm at work."

"You embarrassed one of your friends might see me on your computer screen?"

"No!" she snapped, sounding shocked by the suggestion. "It's just...you and me are a private thing. The guys will tease me if they find out, and Lexi and Chelsea will want to know all the juicy details—and all we're doing is talking. And... and I haven't told my family about you yet. Dad will find out for sure if there's any gossip around here about us."

Why she hadn't told her father and two older brothers about him, he had no clue. Her father, Brian Stockman, was a veteran police officer. Maybe she worried that he'd be overprotective about her getting involved in a new relationship. And Levi had first-hand experience about how over-protective a big brother could be.

But Zoe said none of that.

Levi stroked along Sky's head and back as the big dog stretched out beside him. The contented dog and repetitive strokes soothed enough of the suspicion roiling inside him so that he could keep his tone calm and not escalate this conversation into an argument. "I told you I was fine staying up late so you can chat during the day. I know long-distance isn't an easy way to build a relationship, but we're both hard workers. We don't give up. I thought you wanted to put in the effort. I do."

"You have certain hours you have to be on duty."

He hated that she hadn't immediately responded with an *I do, too.*

But instead of pushing her to agree, he responded to what she had said. "Not twenty-four seven. Not unless we're on lockdown and facing an imminent threat. If you're on the night shift and your free time is during the day, let me be the one to stay up late and lose a couple hours of sleep." He wasn't above begging at this point. "Come on. Please? I love hearing your voice. But I want to see you, too. I miss you. I miss *us*."

"Just the two of us?" she asked.

"Yeah." Sky heaved a deep breath and rolled onto his side, exposing his belly for a tummy rub. "Well, I guess Sky, too. He'll end up wherever I go."

"I'm glad you have Sky. I hope I can meet him in person one day."

"Of course you're going to meet him in person. I've already got the release paperwork started. When I get home—"

"Sorry—I really have to go." He heard a murmur of voices in the background, though none of them were distinct. Then he heard a knock on her office door, and she quickly ran her words together to finish the conversation. "I'm on call tonight, and the team is waiting on me. I'll see what I can do about the FaceTime thing. I'll text or call when I'm available. Pet Sky for me. Stay safe. Goodbye, Levi."

Click. She ended the call.

Goodbye?

How could one simple word sound so ominous?

15 October...

THE NEXT TIME they did meet face-to-face, Levi got the feeling that things weren't improving for Zoe, him or their chance at a future together.

When she appeared on the screen, she was curled up on her couch again. The blanket was pulled up to her shoulders, and all those pink pillows were tucked around her. She hadn't dolled herself up for him—but he didn't mind that. He actually preferred her natural look. Clean, smooth skin. The natural rosy pink of her lips. Long, dark lashes that brushed against the cool alabaster of her skin that revealed every tinge of embarrassment and every flush of passion.

But her beauty tonight was a pale imitation of the woman from his summer encounter who lived in his dreams. Her long hair hung in a limp ponytail over her shoulder. There were visible shadows beneath her eyes, almost making them look bruised. And though he spied the neckline of a thick cable turtleneck, she was shivering.

"Are you sick?" The words were out before he realized he probably should have eased into the question.

The shadow of a smile told him she remembered his blunt way of speaking. "I've felt better," she admitted. "I took a couple of days off. I'm back on call tonight."

That didn't answer his question.

"Did you have a panic attack?" He knew it took her some

time to recover from an episode, especially if it had been bad enough to require her taking medication. She'd said it made her brain fuzzy and it definitely made her sleepy.

"Yeah."

"Did you take one of your pills?" That could explain the fatigue and slight disorientation.

"I can't take them right now."

Probably because she was heading to work.

"What happened?"

Her nostrils flared and her breathing quickened. She brushed her fingers against the laptop screen as if she was caressing his image. But despite the wistful gesture, she didn't elaborate. Her fingers curled into a fist and fell back to her lap.

"Honey, I really need you to talk to me. I'm worried about you."

She was focused on something beyond her laptop—on the coffee table, perhaps. Or maybe her eyes saw nothing at all. "I don't want you to worry. You have enough on your plate already."

"That's what people who care about each other do."

She glanced back toward the computer screen. "But you need to watch your back. Take care of yourself while you're deployed."

"Sky watches my back," he insisted. "I've been doing this Marine thing a long time. I can get the job done *and* worry about you."

"I'm a distraction."

"You're not." Well, she had been. Sure, he could compartmentalize and do his job. But with every missed call, every mail call without a letter, she moved to the front of his thoughts again. "Are you cold? You guys getting an early winter there? I was hoping you'd step outside and show me some fall foliage. Or enclose an autumn leaf in your next letter. Are you getting snow already? I miss the seasons changing."

There was no response. Zoe's lower lip trembled as if she was about to cry. Or crawl out of her skin.

Oh, hell. She wasn't recovering from a panic attack. She was having one right now.

Levi sat at attention. "Babe, look at me." She glanced toward the computer but didn't meet his gaze. When cajoling didn't get her attention on him, he summoned his Master Sergeant voice and clipped a command. "Zoe, eye contact. Please." He ground his teeth together, stemming the concern that wanted to spew out.

There were tears in her eyes when she lifted her gaze. He needed to think like a medic right now, not as a man who loved her. He needed to calm her down.

"Don't zone out on me. Take a deep breath." He pointed to his nose. "Right with me, babe. In through your nose." He held it to the count of five. "And slowly out through your mouth." Her chin shook as she breathed out. "Again." He kept his tone deep and calm and evenly modulated, much as he'd talk to an injured animal or frightened child. "In through the nose. Out through the mouth." There was less trembling this time. "Again. In. Out."

Her unblinking focus zeroed in on his lips. She was concentrating on matching his movements, trusting him to calm her and distract her from the overwhelming emotions. "In. Out."

He watched her visibly calm down as she began to regulate her own breathing. He barely detected her nod that said she was doing better.

"Here." He tapped his thigh, urging Sky to climb onto his lap. "Sky, right." When the German shepherd turned his head, Levi caught him around the jowls and muzzle in some roughhouse petting the dog loved. "Look at this face." Sky's tongue lolled out, and his panting fogged up the screen. "See? You can't cry when you see this face."

The breath she huffed out was almost a laugh. "That's a

goofy face." She reached for the screen. "I wish I could pet him. Would he let me?"

"Yeah," he assured her, knowing Sky would sense her as part of his pack once he understood how important she was to Levi. "Good boy. Get down." He rewarded the dog with some more petting and faced the screen again. "He wouldn't let anybody hurt you. He'd watch over you if you had to shut down for a little while."

Zoe nodded, pressed her lips together, then zeroed in on Levi's gaze. "I wish that I could touch you, too, that I could feel your arms around me. I miss that. You're an anchor for me. I wish that you…" Something in her peripheral vision distracted her. Her frown returned along with her clutch around those pillows. "Sorry about almost losing it. I guess I got overwhelmed."

"By what? What set it off?"

"I'm sorry. I don't want to burden you."

"Don't apologize for being who you are. I told you I was okay with this. You are so smart and intuitive and sensitive and kind that a panic attack doesn't even faze me."

"It should. It's not normal, Levi. *I'm* not normal. How could you possibly want to be with someone like me?"

"How could I not?" He ignored the self-derogatory comment, remembering how he'd helped her get out of her head and move on to a healthier mindset. "It's always going to be the two of us, remember? We're a team. We've got this." He checked the watch on his wrist. "We still have ten minutes. Do you need to talk about what happened? You know I'm a good listener."

"I know." For a moment, he didn't think she was going to explain. But eventually, she started. "I got a letter. Actually… more than one… They…" He heard a phone ringing in the background. Her body stiffened and the color blanched from her face. What the hell? She leaned forward to pick up her phone and breathed an audible sigh of relief. "I need to take this call. It's the lab. I have to go."

"Who did you think was calling?" he snapped, feeling like he was interrogating a prisoner who wouldn't talk. "What letters? From whom? What did they say that upset you? Talk to me."

"It's okay. I'm handling it."

Clearly, she wasn't. "Zoe…"

She waved. "Bye, Sky. Be safe."

"Zo—"

The screen went dark.

What the hell had set off that panic attack? Letters? *His* letters? The stress of finding time when they could be together? Was she starting to rethink him coming home to Kansas City and becoming part of her life?

How had their loving, sometimes funny, always meaningful conversations gotten reduced to polite chats and panic attacks?

Something was wrong. Something had changed.

And he wasn't going to figure it out from eight thousand miles away.

November 1…

LEVI EAGERLY OPENED the envelope with the familiar handwriting he hadn't seen in weeks now. A red oak leaf tumbled out and floated down to his bunk.

Autumn is beautiful in Missouri this year.
Here's the leaf you asked for.
Be safe. —Z

He turned the paper over, expecting to find more. But it wasn't there.

His hand fisted around Zoe's letter, just like the unseen fist squeezing around his heart.

Was something wrong?

He'd had warmer, longer correspondence from the junk mail he sometimes received.

He thought they were getting closer. But now he was feeling like a pen pal, like little more than an afterthought.

Why the hell had Zoe stopped talking to him?

4 November...

HE COULDN'T COMPARTMENTALIZE his emotions as well as he thought after all.

Lying on his stomach in the hospital bed in Germany, with a needle stuck into the back of his hand and an IV tube pumping him full of painkillers and antibiotics, Levi knew he'd screwed up big-time. His thoughts often strayed to Zoe, wondering if he'd misread her interest, worrying that there was something she wasn't telling him, stewing over the distance between them. He'd begun to think that the only way to nurture a relationship and make it work was to be there in person.

That was why he'd gone out of his way two days ago to chat up the young man from the local village that he'd run into several times since being stationed here. Ahmad El Khoury sometimes drove his father's delivery truck, sometimes tagged along to help carry crates, sometimes simply showed up to get away from all his sisters and shoot the breeze or mooch a chocolate bar.

But that morning...

When Ahmad had pulled his father's truck up to the outer gate, the teenager was pale and visibly shaking. The similarity to Zoe's last panic attack pinged Levi's protective instincts and put him on guard. Something was wrong, and Levi wanted to help his young friend—maybe alleviate some of his own frustration and stress at his inability to help Zoe embrace their relationship by helping Ahmad.

He squirmed on the pillows tucked beneath his chest and

ankles, trying to find a more comfortable position. In addition to the pain knifing through his lower back and the backs of his shoulders and legs, his thoughts kept him awake. Twenty years in the Corps and he'd made a dumb mistake a private fresh out of basic would never make.

He'd dropped his guard.

Sky had detected one IED in an unloaded crate, and the team had reacted just as they'd been trained: Clear the area. Contain the threat. Detain the suspect. Then call in an Explosive Ordnance Disposal technician to disassemble or dispose of the bomb. Levi's men had given the EOD tech the space they needed.

As he escorted Ahmad toward the detention area, gently pressing the nervous teen for information—Did he know about the bomb? Had he been coerced into transporting it? Did he know who put it there?—Levi had dismissed Sky's frantic whining. Maybe the dog was still pumped with adrenaline after his successful search. Maybe there was a trace scent of explosive on the young man's clothes after loading the back of the truck.

Levi had been so hell-bent on helping the teen, on proving his innocence, on protecting him from local political factions who'd forced him to carry a bomb that he'd missed the obvious. Ahmad stopped, pulled up the hem of his dishdasha and showed him the secondary device strapped around his waist. The boy was in tears, but that didn't change the damn fact that Levi had ignored his training and ignored his canine partner who was never wrong when it came to trouble.

Ahmad had apologized, then muttered, "Run."

Shouting orders to his teammates, Levi had hauled Sky up into his arms and ran.

He remembered the concussive noise, the whoosh of hot air that had lifted him off his feet, the scorching heat of the blast as fire rained down around him.

Levi squeezed his eyes shut against the memories and dropped his hand over the edge of the bed to touch the thick, warm fur of Sky's flank as the wounded dog rested on the makeshift bed on the floor beside him. Screw hospital regulations. Apparently, neither dog nor Marine had calmed down enough without sedation until they were reunited again. The moment he felt his handler's touch, Sky lifted his head and touched his cold, wet nose to Levi's wrist.

The dog licked Levi's hand as he reached inside the protective cone that kept the dog from licking his injuries and petted him around his head and muzzle. "I'm sorry I didn't listen, Sky. You were right. You were a good boy."

Neither of their injuries were life-threatening unless they became infected. That was only because his safety gear and body had taken the brunt of the explosion. But the shrapnel cuts had needed stitches, and the burns had needed repeated debriding, removal of dead skin and several applications of a nasty-smelling goop.

Ahmad had been the only casualty in the explosion.

That and Levi's conscience.

When Sky lay back down to rest, Levi dropped his head and listened to the sounds of the darkened base hospital. Some distant beeps of machines; some low, indistinct voices from the nurse's station down the hallway; Sky's relaxed breathing. Man, this was a lonely place to be stuck with his thoughts.

The men and woman on his security team had been by to check on him and Sky before he'd been flown to Germany. Through a fog of painkillers, he'd listened to the full incident report and was grateful that no one else had been injured badly enough to be evacuated from the base hospital. But he and Sky were still alone.

Distracted by his disintegrating relationship and the raw wounds on his skin, Levi decided to be a glutton for punishment and picked up his cell phone from the table beside his bed.

He needed to talk to someone. He needed Zoe's patience and gentleness to soothe him.

She hadn't instigated any contact with him since that letter with the autumn leaf. Not one text just to say *I miss you* or to tell him *Be safe*.

He pressed her name, but she didn't answer his call. The number didn't even ring but went straight to voicemail. Without bothering to leave a message, he ended the call and texted her instead.

Hey, babe. In case you're interested, I got hurt. Sky, too. Not enough to get shipped home, but enough to put us out of commission in the hospital for a few weeks. I sure could use someone to talk to.

It was foolish of him to expect three dots to pop up on his screen, indicating an instant response from her. He rubbed his hand over his scruffy beard and cursed the silence, trying to understand why she was ghosting him.

Levi waited.

Nothing.

Nothing.

And then a message popped up.

This number is no longer in service.

"What the hell?" Pain shot through his back and limbs as every muscle in him tensed up. She'd changed her number without telling him? Now he felt like some kind of stalker, some creep who made her uncomfortable enough that she had to disconnect him from her life.

Levi tapped the IV tube to give himself another dose of meds to mellow out his anger and take the edge off his pain.

Then he breathed deeply through his nose, pushing his emotions aside and willing logical thought to center himself again.

Could be that Zoe had lost her phone. Maybe winter had come early to Missouri and she'd dropped her cell into a snow drift. She probably had it sitting in a bowl of rice, trying to dry it out. Maybe she'd been inundated with spam calls and texts, so she'd gotten rid of it. Maybe the disconnect was as simple as a decision to go with a new service provider, and she hadn't had a chance to update him with the new information.

Then again, maybe he was the thing that upset her, so she'd changed her number. Maybe Levi had been nothing more than a brief summer fling to her, while he'd been thinking long-term. Maybe he'd simply been an easy escape from the stress and anxiety that had consumed her that Fourth of July.

After all, the teenager who had blown himself up at the base's front gate proved Levi wasn't as good at reading people as he'd thought he was.

He rolled onto his side to give his back a break from lying in the awkward position. He looked down over the edge of the bed at Sky. "I miss her, big guy. I just need her to say hi. I need her to tell me that we're gonna be okay."

Big brown eyes looked up at him in sympathy.

"We're both gonna look different with these scars. She may not think I'm so hot anymore." A wry chuckle tickled his throat. "Maybe she already thinks that. Bet that's why she's ghosting us." He hadn't even realized that his eyes were burning until a tear spilled over and dripped onto his pillow. Tears? Hell. He swiped them away with the back of his hand. "I thought she was good for us, bud. I thought we were good for her." Instead, he felt left behind, abandoned. "It's you and me, Sky. Like always."

Sky whined and sat up. The dog's IV had been removed. But the nicks where the shrapnel had pierced his thick fur and then been stitched up and bandaged, and the road rash on his front right paw where Levi had landed on him and they'd skidded into the curb surrounding the guard house made the powerful, athletic dog move like an old man. Levi knew the feeling. Still, gritting his teeth against the stretch of muscles and skin, he helped the dog climb onto the bed beside him. He needed that connection—that warmth, that loyalty, that unquestionable trust—right now. He hugged his arm around Sky and rested his head on the pillow beside the dog's black muzzle.

"Just the two of us."

OH, THIS WAS just too perfect.

One of the pictures fell out of the photographer's coat and landed in the grave atop the Popsicle of a corpse that had kept remarkably well in the industrial freezer where she'd been stored for three months now. Although the urge to retrieve the photograph was strong, because the collection would now be incomplete, it might add an interesting twist once the body was discovered and the authorities at KCPD realized the brunette college student hadn't been a random attack.

Because it had become abundantly clear that simply killing the young woman lacked the impact necessary for completing the plan. There needed to be a bigger twist, a better story to report.

The photographer scooped up another shovel of dirt and debris and spread it over the picture and the plastic-wrapped body beneath it.

Taking this one had been remarkably easy. It was just a matter of studying the target long enough to know everything about her. What was important to her? What was she afraid of? When and where was she most vulnerable? Attack her after mental anguish and self-doubts had torn her down and taken away her power. Make her easy prey.

Then all one had to do was act like a normal person, become part of her world in such a way that she'd never suspect the threat staring her in the face until it was too late. The photographer had learned from the best.

Taking the college student had been good practice. But it was time to up the game. With bigger risks came bigger rewards. And who wouldn't want the reward the photographer would soon earn?

The real target was within their grasp. A happily-ever-after would soon be theirs.

Chapter Three

Thanksgiving Day...

For twenty years, the family tradition had been for Levi to call home from wherever he was in the world to share the holiday with his little sister. This year was no different.

He wasn't going to contact Zoe. He hadn't heard from her with an updated phone number, and she'd never answered any of his emails. He'd written out a four-page letter to send her but had ended up stuffing it into his duffel bag because it had been filled with anger.

Relationships ended. He knew that. But he was never going to find out why Zoe had ended theirs until he could talk to her face-to-face. Today he was going to treat himself to family time before heading over to the mess tent for turkey and mashed potatoes and about six different kinds of pie.

Levi sat in the communications room and waited for Lexi's picture to appear onscreen. When the picture came on and filled the screen, he grinned from ear to ear.

Lexi Callahan-Murphy was a slighter, feminine version of Levi. They shared the same green eyes and light brown hair, although hers had more blond in it. She showcased the family's natural curls with her chin-length hairstyle, while he kept his cropped too short to curl. He was equally pleased to see his dark-haired brother-in-law and best friend, Aiden, trying to contain the fussy toddler with her daddy's blue-black hair and green eyes from the Callahan side of the family. A Belgian Malinois woofed in the background, and he recognized Aiden's K-9 partner, Blue.

"Happy Thanksgiving," he said, enjoying the true picture of a young, loving family. "Good to see you guys."

He smiled through the chorus of greetings that ended with Rose scrambling over Aiden's shoulder, muttering, "Top. Top. Top."

Between *Levi*, *Uncle* and *Sergeant*, it was the one word Rose had been able to pronounce, and had therefore latched onto, when he'd been home that summer. He'd take the nickname. He loved that she knew who he was.

"Looks like you've got your hands full there, Aiden," Levi teased. "You beatin' boys off with a stick yet?"

Aiden sighed and pulled the girl back onto his lap. "That's the one thing I haven't had to do yet. She's walking, climbing out of her crib, rolling around in the snow with Blue. I'm sure she'll be getting into something new tomorrow." When she tried to lower herself off the sofa between where her parents were sitting, Aiden scooped her up again. "I know I was a handful growing up and probably deserve a firecracker like Rosie, but I kind of figured she'd be a little older before she started giving me grief."

"You love it," Levi answered.

Aiden winked. "You know I do. Never had a family until I met the Callahans. I love helping it grow."

His sister gazed lovingly at Aiden and Rose, and Levi felt a pang of jealousy. He'd imagined something similar between him and Zoe. But he was beginning to think he'd been the only one imagining that.

Aiden picked up the little girl and stood, hunching down to stay in the picture. "Hey, bro, I just wanted to see for myself that you were in one piece. I'll let you talk to Lexi while I corral the dog and our little adventuress." He leaned down to kiss Lexi's temple before doffing a salute to the screen. "We'll see you in a month. Listen to Sky. And don't scare your sister like that again," he chided, sending the message that they'd both been worried about him getting wounded.

"Do my best." Levi promised. "Blue, you watch his back. See you soon."

Once they were alone, Lexi picked up her laptop, metaphorically pulling him closer, and settled it onto her lap. "You look good. Better than the last time we talked. How is your recovery going?"

"Things are scarring up. They've got me back on light duty to finish out my assignment."

"And Sky?"

"He's healing faster than me." He called the German shepherd up to get his long black muzzle and dark eyes in the camera shot so his sister could see. He held up the dog's right front paw. "He wears a bootie now to keep the newly healed skin from getting irritated or breaking open again. He wears it as well as his harness and vest. But he misses the routine. I've been doing regular training sessions with him, but downtime is not his best thing."

"It's not your best thing, either." She shook her finger at him. "I'm guessing you're trying to do more than the doctor says you're supposed to." She arched an eyebrow, daring him to deny it. "Are you in any pain?"

"The new skin is still a little tender, but nothing major."

"And your sessions with the counselor? Isn't the young man who died the same one you wanted to sponsor so he could come here and go to college?"

"Yeah."

"I'm sorry, Levi."

"Me, too." He blinked his sight into focus before his sister could figure out just how messed up he was inside. "Hey, what can you tell me about Zoe Stockman? Is she still your twin science geek at the lab?"

"Zoe?"

Yeah, that had come out of left field. He hadn't told Lexi that he and Zoe were a thing. Had been a thing?

He saw a smile of excitement at first. Lexi had long been trying to match him up with someone. But that smile had quickly turned into a frown of confusion. "Where'd you hear that *twin science geek* line? That's what the guys at the lab call us."

"Is she okay?" he asked, needing to know that at least.

"As far as I know. I worry about her not eating enough." Lexi frowned. "Is there something I should be worried about?"

"I was hoping you could tell me."

Lexi sat up straight on the couch and put on her mystery-solving expression. "Levi, are you okay? I mean, this is a weird conversation."

"Is it?" He absently stroked the top of Sky's head.

"Yeah. I didn't know you were friends with Zoe."

Zoe hadn't mentioned him to his sister at all? Maybe she was uncomfortable talking about private matters with her supervisor. He nodded. "We're friends." He'd thought it was something more, but maybe that had been wishful thinking on his part. "We met at the Fourth of July party at your place. We hit it off."

He could see her processing her memories. "That's right. You both disappeared before the fireworks were over."

"Yeah, we went for a long walk and…talked. We were communicating pretty regularly until a few weeks ago. I've got some time on my hands, and I thought I'd check in. But apparently she's changed her number. Maybe I misread the vibe between us."

"The vibe?"

"Yeah." *You know, the vibe telling me I finally found the one?* But he'd been wrong. "We talked," he repeated lamely.

"That must have been some conversation."

Levi shifted uncomfortably. He wasn't used to lying to his sister. "I'm half a world away, kiddo. And I'm not psychic. I can't reach her. I was hoping you could tell me what's going on with her."

"I'm glad you're interested. She needs a good friend right about now."

That sounded suspicious. "Why does she need a friend?"

"Well, for starters, her dad was in a pretty serious accident with his truck. He's home now, on crutches, but won't be back to work until the beginning of the year. It was pretty scary to get that phone call. Zoe took a week off to take care of him, and she's still checking on him regularly. But with everything she's got going on, it's taken a toll on her."

He did not like the sound of that. "What happened?"

"He lost control of the vehicle and ran into a tree. Broke both his legs." She sighed. "I probably shouldn't tell you this since it's an ongoing case, but his brake lines had been tampered with. Sergeant Stockman has been a cop for a long time, so we're guessing it's payback from some criminal he put away. But we don't have any leads."

Levi squeezed his hands into fists. His instinct was to find Zoe—to hold her, to take some of the burden of worry from her—but he didn't even know her phone number anymore. "She didn't ask any of you for help?"

"You know how she keeps to herself. She's never been the same since her relationship with Ethan Wynn. I suppose finding out that you've fallen in love with a serial killer probably makes you second-guess your choices in men. In life, too, maybe."

"I'm glad Aiden and Blue took Wynn down. That man has ruined enough lives."

"Hey, I had a hand in helping with that conviction."

"I know you did, kiddo," he teased, understanding that she wanted to lighten the mood and not dwell on the traitor in their own crime lab who'd tried to kill her more than once. "Wynn never stood a chance against the three of you working together."

She smiled, and he breathed a sigh of relief. "At any rate, I think Zoe keeps to herself a lot because she probably feels guilty for not realizing how evil Ethan was and how he'd insinuated himself into all our lives at the lab. Maybe she feels she should have warned me? I'm sure he preyed on her insecurities."

Yeah, they'd had that conversation, too, about the mind games her ex had played on Zoe. "There's no way she could know how messed up in the head that loser was. She thought he was her mentor and protector, and he took advantage of that. In the end, he scared her, too."

"I know that." Lexi tucked her hair behind her ears and smiled sympathetically. "Even with her father working here, she hasn't gotten close to any of us. Keeps her private life very private. She's a damn fine criminalist. I'd love to talk shop with her more often. Any of us are happy to work with her, but she hasn't warmed up to anyone beyond work relationships. So, yeah, I hope she has some friends outside of the crime lab. She could use a big brother like you in her life."

Big brother? His feelings for Zoe had never been brotherly. "She already has two big brothers."

"You know what I mean. You're my hero. You made sure we stayed together as a family when we lost Mom and Dad. I know what kind of man you are—your sense of duty and honor, your big heart—the way you never shy away from responsibility and doing the right thing. Any woman would be lucky to have you as a friend." Her brows arched with speculation. "Or something more?"

He wasn't going to get into the mess he'd made of his love life. Not on a holiday. And not with his sister. "If you see her, let her know I've been trying to reach out to her. She can call or text or even write a letter. I'd really like to hear from her."

"I'll make sure she gets the message."

"Thanks, sis."

Their conversation turned to some remodeling they were doing on the house and, ultimately, to his niece, Rose, who had just celebrated her first birthday.

While he loved his family and hearing all about them, Levi's thoughts kept straying back to Zoe.

She needs a good friend right about now.

What was wrong with Zoe?

Why did she no longer want Levi's help?

Or his heart?

December...

It was Zoe's voice on the phone. "You got hurt? Lexi filled me in at work yesterday. Are you all right? Why didn't you tell me?"

"Because we haven't been talking to each other lately." He almost hadn't answered the call because he didn't recognize the number. But a part of him had hoped she was finally reaching out to him—the same part that wanted to kick himself for snapping at her. "How's your dad?"

"Dad?" She seemed surprised that he knew about the accident. "He's on the mend. He has enough pins in his legs to set off the metal detector at the airport, and he's using crutches instead of his wheelchair most of the time now. But I want to talk about you."

"Why? Why now? I've been here the whole time. Are you just now feeling guilty about ditching me?"

He could tell his tone had stung because she hesitated to

continue the conversation. But then she sniffled a quick breath, making him think she was crying, and he felt even worse. "I'm sorry. When your sister mentioned it—that you'd been in an explosion—I wanted to call you right away. I wanted to put my hands on you and see you with my own eyes. I think you're the kind of man who would lie about how badly he's hurt because you'd be worried about upsetting me. Dad's been the same way. I'm not fragile, Levi. I'm...okay. When my focus is outward, I'm not fragile. Please tell me you're all right."

Brave, he decided. Despite her challenges, she pushed forward every damn day to do her job, to be with people, to put up with his moods. Still felt like too little, too late.

"I don't want your pity, Zoe. Yeah, I'm going to have a few scars. I'm not that handsome guy you went to bed with."

"Are. You. All. Right?"

He was the one who needed to take a deep breath and deal with her out-of-the-blue phone call. "They kept Sky and me in the hospital in Germany for a few weeks. Did a lot of skin treatments on me. But they determined I could finish out my tour of duty instead taking a medical discharge since I was so close to being out."

"Sky was hurt, too?" Her sad gasp tugged at heartstrings he didn't want to feel anymore. "I bet you felt worse about that than getting hurt yourself."

She was the first person to figure that out. But he'd needed those words—he'd needed this comfort—earlier. He'd hardened himself to the idea of him and Zoe having any kind of happily-ever-after.

"Levi? Are you still there?"

"They didn't muster out Sky, either. Gave us both a clean bill of health as long as we stick to light duty and I show up for my regular treatments."

"What happened? Or do you not want to talk about it?"

Levi tipped his head back and exhaled a hot breath into the

darkened barracks. "I've wanted to talk about a lot of things these past few months, Zoe. Find out what happened to your dad. Ask why you don't make friends at the crime lab. Make plans for our future. But you changed your number on me. I took that to mean you weren't interested—"

"That's not true. I didn't change it because of you. I needed *him* to stop…" The *him* should have registered, should have worried Levi. But he wasn't in the mood to ask, and she wasn't willing to explain. "I've had…stuff…to deal with."

"Well, babe, you just go on dealing with your *stuff* all on your own. I'll deal with mine."

"Levi, I need to tell you something. But I don't want you to be mad when I tell you. And you sound like you're already mad."

"You don't want me to be mad? How do you expect me to feel when you keep blowing me off?"

She sounded surprised by that. "I've been completely stressed. I haven't even told my dad everything. I didn't want him to worry. I don't want you to worry. I'm trying to protect—"

"I'm sorry, Zoe. I can't do this right now. My blood pressure is rising, and I need to hit the gym or take Sky for a run."

"It's the middle of the night there."

He swung his legs over the side of his bunk. Sleep would be a nonstarter tonight. He might as well get some exercise. "I need to go."

"Oh. Okay. I don't want to make anything worse. But we *do* need to talk. Wh…when you're ready. But soon."

He thought he detected the telltale signs of her fighting the instinctive urge to shut down. "I don't want you to feel sorry for me, Zo. You either decide you want the two of us to be a thing—or you don't."

"Please don't put that pressure on me. I can't right now. I need—"

"You decide. And then we'll talk."

15 December...

LEVI'S ULTIMATUM HAD backfired on him big-time.

He'd been so frustrated by Zoe's silence. So hurt that she hadn't cared enough to make contact until she'd found out he'd been injured that it had eaten away the trust he'd had in her.

You decide. And then we'll talk.

That was why he was pacing the locker room at the gym with Sky following dutifully on his heels at zero dark thirty when he finally sank down onto a bench and pulled out his cell phone. He knew she'd be starting her day at work at the crime lab, but he prayed she'd see his message and pick up anyway.

He was at the end of his rope. He needed her to understand. He needed her to forgive his anger. He needed her.

He carefully typed out his text.

I'm getting out in two weeks. When I get home to KC, I want to see you.

No response.

I can come by, or we can meet somewhere. Have that talk. Your call. Let me know.

Zoe?

Zo?

Sky panting at his feet gave him more of an answer than he was getting from Zoe.

He took a risk and pulled up her new contact information on the Call screen and pressed her number.

Her voicemail kicked on. Nearly eight thousand miles across the world and all he had to talk to was her damn voicemail.

"Zoe, I know you have panic attacks. I'm cool with that—you know I am. I'm a patient man—at least, I used to be," he amended honestly. "But I never thought you were a coward. If you don't want anything to do with me anymore…if you've found someone else or you don't want to be with a man in uniform who can't be there twenty-four seven, three-sixty-five, and who got himself a little messed up while over here…if my talk about settling down scared you off…if you're dumping me, have the courtesy to tell me to my face. At least send me a damn Dear John letter so I know not to hope. I thought we were real. I thought we were gonna last."

He paused, then decided to say the words he'd never uttered before. "I loved you, Zo. Like I've never loved anyone else before. Now I just want answers. Believe me, when I get home, I intend to get them. Be prepared for that conversation. I hope you're safe and well. Callahan out."

THIS LETTER MEANT EVERYTHING.

Approval. Promise. Affirmation that the goal the photographer wanted was in reach.

Things in the master plan were moving along just the way they were meant to be. As long as there were no unforeseen complications, a happily-ever-after should be guaranteed.

Zoe Stockmann was proving to be the perfect target. So broken. So alone. So afraid to reach out for help. So satisfying to see how she suffered despite bravely waking up each day and trying to live her life, as if she was a normal person, as if she mattered. But Zoe was just a pawn in a carefully mapped-out game. Soon her bravery would falter and eventually she'd surrender to the inevitable. Her destruction and death would be the culmination of months of hard work, planning and patience. And the reward would be everything that the photographer had ever wanted.

Smiling, the photographer carefully folded the letter and replaced it in its envelope.

Then the photographer got comfortable in their seat, raised the camera and starting snapping pictures of the dark-haired beauty who'd been chosen to make every dream come true.

Chapter Four

Zoe's breath steamed up the floor-to-ceiling window in the main hallway of the Kansas City Crime Lab as she watched snowflakes drift down to join the three inches of snow that had already blown in on Christmas Eve.

"You're probably out there right now, aren't you," she whispered, pressing her hand against the cool glass, wishing she could be on the other side of the window, breathing in the crisp air. But she felt eyes on her all the time. Some of that feeling of being under someone's microscope was probably her own paranoia, part of her anxiety. But not all of it. Not by a long shot. "Something else you've stolen from me."

Normally, she'd be out there in the wintry landscape. She loved the snow and the cold, found it fun and invigorating and beautiful when it first fell. She enjoyed playing in the snow and had even made a snow angel and built a snowman in her father's backyard last Christmas. She loved the beauty and quiet serenity of hiking in snowshoes and even driving out to the farmland outside the city to see the vast swaths of undisturbed snow glistening across the rolling landscape, unmarred by city snowplows, crusty salt nuggets and dirty slush. The damp, bracing air energized her. The miracle of every single unique snowflake inspired her. Snow made her happy.

She'd even managed to lose her heart to a man who loved the snow and cold as much as she did. Of course, Levi Callahan's fascination with snow might've had more to do with all the years he'd been stationed in desert or tropical duty stations than with any shared interest he had with her. She wasn't sure she shared much of anything in common with Levi anymore, not after the way she'd been forced to treat him these past few months.

Her hand drifted down to the front of her oversized lab coat. Well, they shared one thing. And he didn't even know it. No one except her ob-gyn and her father knew her secret.

Running on a skeleton crew between the Christmas and New Year's holidays, the crime lab's vast maze of hallways, labs and offices felt extra empty and lonely. But she couldn't go out and breathe in the reviving cold air. She couldn't dredge up her inner child and make a snowball and splat it against a tree.

Outside wasn't safe. Outside wasn't hers to enjoy anymore.

Her world had become very small and very frightening.

I never thought you were a coward.

Levi's words cut through Zoe like a hot poker.

Maybe she *was* a coward. Afraid to leave the building. Afraid to indulge her love of winter. Afraid to share her secret with anyone close to her—afraid to *let* anyone get too close. Afraid to seize the love she'd so briefly found with a patient, protective, rugged Marine this past summer.

Afraid, afraid, afraid.

She reached inside her white lab coat to touch the front of her pinned-together baggy jeans. She really needed to invest in some maternity clothes. But shopping by herself didn't feel particularly safe when she knew she was being watched. Plus, she'd risk advertising her pregnancy just by walking into the maternity department or having a delivery made to her front door. And she didn't want the rest of the world to know about the baby before she told Levi.

And she certainly didn't want *him* to know.

How to Hurt Zoe.

She had the words from the very first letter memorized. They'd been a textbook example of how a stalker could isolate her and drive everything that mattered from her life.

She cupped her hand around her lower belly where she felt flutters of movement. But not this. Never this. *He* would never get his hands on her baby. Her instincts told her to shield this small life with everything she had in her. But she wanted to share every new discovery and celebrate the child growing inside her, too. The doctor had said the fluttering was normal—the first signs of movement. The baby was too small to truly kick yet. But sometimes at night, when she was lying down, it felt like popcorn kernels popping. She smiled at the memory, longing to call Levi or a friend, if she ever made one, and share each miraculous sensation.

But she couldn't do that. She couldn't share her excitement or ask advice or even enjoy a shopping trip or a day in the snow.

Some of her doom and gloom had to do with hormones that had been seriously out of whack for weeks now. But most of it had to do with the letter in her pocket. One of several that had shown up like clockwork every week since the end of August. She'd dusted this morning's letter for prints—like usual, there were none—and planned to run a DNA test if she could find a usable sample. But the sender seemed to know all the same tricks a criminalist would use to process evidence, and *he'd* made sure there was nothing she could tag to identify the anonymous notes.

This morning's letter she'd found tucked beneath the windshield wiper of her car had been addressed the same as always: *To Zoe Stockmann.* She wanted to attach some significance to the fact that *he* kept adding an extra *n* to the end of her name. But it probably didn't mean anything except that *he* hadn't aced spelling class. The message inside was a variation on a theme.

Didn't you like my Christmas present?

I asked you to hang it up in your window where I could see it.

I don't see it.

I don't like it when you disobey me.

Who shall I hurt this time? Who's next on my list? One of your brothers? Your niece? The cute young man with the beard I saw you with at the last crime scene?

Another brunette who is a pale imitation of your beauty?

The accident that could have killed her dad was the wake-up call that finally made her realize how real and how deadly the threat against her was. Against her brothers and their families. Against the people she worked with. Against her. Against the baby, too, if *he* ever found out.

There'd been gifts at her doorstep. Pictures of her. So many pictures that she suspected *he* was always watching—at home, at the lab, at crime scenes, even at the grocery store and gas station where she stopped on her way home from work. Maybe *he'd* set up surveillance at the places she'd frequented most so that *he* could remotely monitor her twenty-four seven. She'd discovered a tracking device on her car and had removed it, bagged it as evidence and reported it to Lexi. But there'd been a new tracker on her car the next day, along with a warning that if she tampered with any of *his* gifts ever again *he'd* make her pay for her ingratitude. That same day, her father's truck had been sabotaged, and he could have died.

She curled both arms around her middle now. *He* wasn't hurting this baby.

The only time she'd been in a relationship with anyone who showed this kind of obsession had been when she'd dated her former mentor, Ethan Wynn. But Ethan was in prison now, serving subsequent life sentences for killing three women and attempting to kill a fourth—her supervisor, Lexi Callahan-Murphy.

Because Zoe had testified against him, Ethan wasn't allowed to contact her. He couldn't call her, couldn't write. He certainly couldn't waltz about Kansas City dropping off gifts and surveilling her. Ethan's cousin, Arlo Wynn, had called her a few times over the past three years, usually when he was drunk, to berate her for helping put his cousin in prison, for not being a loyal girlfriend and providing him with an alibi and, in general, being a lousy excuse for a woman. She'd done a little investigating on her own and had learned that Arlo was a vagabond who skirted the law with misdemeanor crimes. He'd lived all across the country, including a stint for several months as Ethan's roommate in Kansas City when she'd first met him. Had Arlo come back to Kansas City to torment her? Maybe at the behest of Ethan?

With her lousy track record for relationships, she shouldn't be surprised that she'd picked up a stalker. Maybe this wasn't related to Ethan at all. She'd smiled at the wrong person or testified against someone in court on another case or…what?

The one exception was the week she'd met Levi Callahan. She'd known he was good. That he was trustworthy. That he was caring and kind and patient. That he was strong and sexy and the most remarkable lover she'd ever had. He listened. He made her laugh. And though he must've outweighed her by at least a hundred pounds, he was gentle and sweet, and he made her feel safe.

And she'd had to give that up.

To protect him, to protect herself, to protect their baby.

I loved you, Zo. Like I've never loved anyone else before.

Past tense. Levi's message cut through her like a whip stripping skin off her body. He didn't love her anymore. She'd done what she had to do without telling him why. He deserved better. She should have been able to handle this whole situation better. But she hadn't. And Levi was hurting and angry because of it.

Tears stung her eyes, and she quickly swiped them away when her phone rang.

She pulled her cell phone from her pocket and answered. "Hello?"

"Jordan Fletcher here. *Kansas City Journal.* Crime-beat reporter. Remember me, Ms. Stockman?" His perkiness alone on this gloomy day, filled with gloomy thoughts, was reason enough to dread his phone calls.

"Of course I remember you, Mr. Fletcher. How can I help you?"

"Jordan, please. And may I call you Zoe?" He continued on without giving her a chance to respond. "I was calling for an update on the Emily Hartman case. Haven't heard any new developments on her disappearance for a while. I tried calling you a couple of times, but you've changed your phone. I had to call in a favor to get your new number."

"Call in a favor? From whom?" She hadn't given her new number to that many people. Just family and a handful of friends and coworkers.

The reporter laughed. "I can't divulge my sources. It's in the constitution."

"No, it's not, actually." Several states had press laws, but Missouri wasn't one of them. Still, she wasn't about to tell a reporter looking for a hot story that she'd gotten a new phone to protect herself from a stalker. "I just… I don't give my number out to many people."

"Well, I'm glad to be one of the few, then."

"But I didn't—"

"Look, this Emily Hartman thing has really fired up the city. A college student disappears from the parking lot behind her apartment and hasn't been seen for months? The whole city is drawing together like a small town, with everybody looking for any sign of Emily. Especially with it being the holidays."

"Yes, it's very tragic."

"So…are there any new leads? Do you think she's been sex trafficked? Maybe she's not even in the states anymore. Are you and the police looking for a body now?"

Zoe was shocked by where this conversation was going. "You can't print anything like that. We don't know."

"Yeah, yeah. She's been missing almost six months now. There was blood found at the abduction site. Don't you think she's dead?"

There had only been a trace amount of blood. Possibly from a blow to subdue the woman, or perhaps where she'd fallen and hit the pavement during the attack. Zoe paused at the leading question, feeling sick to her stomach in a way that had nothing to do with morning sickness. "Not enough blood for her to have died there," she vaguely corrected the reporter. "Until we find a body, we're treating this as if she's still—"

"Don't give me the party line, Zoe." Jordan huffed a sigh, sounding disappointed in her. "When we talked at the abduction site, I knew Emily's case was personal for you. You're only a few years older than she was. You two look alike. You both live alone."

"How do you know…?"

"I could tell this case was personal because you could see yourself in Emily."

What? She wasn't a kidnapping victim. She wasn't a victim. She… She clasped her free hand to her chest, feeling her heart racing. Did she identify with Emily Hartman? Was she worried that she'd be abducted, too? Had *he* tormented Emily before she disappeared? Was that the same game *he* was playing with her now?

While the rising panic squeezed the air from her lungs, Jordan continued. "That's why I want to tell this story through your eyes, from your point of view. This is a national issue. You're fighting for Emily, for yourself, for every vulnerable young woman who lives with the fear of being targeted, of being overpowered. A woman's fear for her personal safety is the daily battle I want to tap into."

"I… You can't…exploit…" She wasn't about to become the poster child for women's safety. She'd worked too hard to regain her strength and some self-assurance after Ethan. And she would do it again—for her baby, for her family, for everyone she cared about. But before she could find the words, the soft beeping from her watch pulled Zoe from her morbid thoughts. She tapped the screen to silence the timer. Her test should have run and been completed by now. "Sorry, Mr. Fletcher, er, Jordan. I just had some time-sensitive tests finish up, and I need to examine and document the results."

"I'll let you go, then. But you still have my card, right?"

She supposed it was still stuck in a side pocket of her crime-scene kit. "I think so."

"Good. If not, you can always just redial this number. Put me in your contacts list." Right. Maybe she'd do that just so she'd recognize his number and didn't have to answer again. "You know, my offer to make you the face of the KCPD Crime Lab and their successes still stands. You're very photogenic."

"Thank you. But my answer is the same—I'm not interested."

"It'd be your chance to put a positive spin on all the good work the crime lab is doing to help solve cases."

"We're background players, Jordan. We build solid cases

to back up the investigations the police are conducting. I... I don't want to be front-page news."

"If you find Emily, you'll let me know?" She envisioned him smiling. "A picture's worth a thousand words."

"I'd never let you take a picture of a murder victim for your paper."

"Of course not. But I could snap photos of the crime scene and you and your team working to solve the case."

"I really do have to go. Goodbye." She hung up without another word and pocketed her phone.

It was hard to imagine anything more unsettling than starring in Jordan Fletcher's newspaper column or using a victim like Emily Hartman to sell papers and promote his career.

Concentrating on work should help her keep her fears in check. She wiped the dampness off the window with the rolled-up cuff of the men's-sized white lab coat she'd borrowed to hide her changing figure. Then she slipped into the memorial lounge at the end of the hallway to make herself a fresh mug of green tea and headed back around the corner into the interior of the building where the labs were located.

She set her tea on the long stainless-steel table and scanned the information on the computer screen and laptop in front of her. After confirming the results of the substance identification—desiccated toothpaste—from the backpack that the missing college student whose case she'd been working the past few months, Zoe sighed and groaned in frustration. "Probably carried a tube in her bag for those days when she went straight from classes to work or a date night."

She'd hoped it would be some kind of plaster or construction residue that would indicate where the young woman had been so that the police could retrace her steps. But then Zoe looked over at the photograph from the alleged abduction site. She remembered that she'd scraped that substance from the *outside* of the student's backpack. The contents of the bag had been dumped outside the girl's car—books, keys, glasses, even her wallet. The money and a credit card had been stolen, but the ID was still there. And there'd been no sign of any toiletries, not even a toothbrush, much less a tube of toothpaste.

"Were you a slob?" she speculated, then quickly dismissed the idea as she scrolled through pictures of the woman's car and apartment. "You're as neat as I am." And Zoe liked to be organized.

She looked back at the sample. "So, whose toothpaste are you?"

Zoe typed up the results of the test and saved it in the case file. She'd run it through DNA next.

After packing up the evidence from the missing-person case and returning it to the evidence locker, she came back to her laptop. She was checking the FBI's Automated Fingerprint Identification System for a more personal reason. She'd found no matches in the crime lab's local database, so she'd expanded the search to the national level. She stared at the print she was running, wondering if she'd retrieved enough of a clean sample to even find the match. She opened the file of prints she'd taken from her father's truck after his so-called accident, wondering if she'd overlooked a clearer print.

Zoe was so engrossed in her work that she startled at the knock at the lab's door. She pressed a hand to her racing heart and forced herself to take a calming breath as her boss strolled in.

"Sorry to startle you." Lexi walked up to the opposite side of the tall table and leaned against it. "It's almost five o'clock, Zoe. What are you still doing here?"

"Running some more tests on the Emily Hartman case." She turned the monitor around to show her supervisor. "That substance I found on her backpack is toothpaste. Based on everything else at the crime scene, though, I'm guessing it's not hers."

"You think it belongs to her abductor?"

"If it's hers, DNA will prove it. If not, it might lead us to someone else the police could question. Someone who saw her shortly before she disappeared, or a man in her life we don't know about."

Lexi nodded, approving her reasoning. "That's as good a lead as anything we've had so far." She cleared her throat and offered Zoe an apologetic smile. "I got another call from that reporter, Jordan Fletcher, this morning, following up to see if we'd made any progress on the investigation. I think he believed covering Emily Hartman's abduction was going to put him on the front page of the *Journal*. Earn him a Pulitzer, from the way he's dogging us about it."

Zoe cringed. "Yeah. I just got off the phone with him. He thinks we should be treating Emily as a murder victim, not a missing person. I didn't confirm anything or share any of our test results."

"Good. I'm not particularly thrilled that he's singled out this case—or that he's singled out you to be his information source."

"He's relentless." Jordan Fletcher contacted her almost as regularly as her stalker did. At least he didn't use some electronic device to distort his voice into sounding like a creepy robot. "He said he called in a favor to get my new phone number. I don't know who helped him."

"You changed your number because of Fletcher?" Lexi pushed away from the table, looking like she was about to go all protective Mama Bear on the reporter. "Was he harassing you that much?"

The easy answer would be to just say yes. The problem was she didn't know who kept calling and leaving her notes and gifts she didn't want. The voice on the phone was mechanically distorted. The messages were printed, not handwritten, making them harder to trace. If Jordan Fletcher *was* behind the harassment campaign, then he'd never get another interview with her.

There were men with persistence—and then there was stalking.

Some sixth sense in her knew…feared…dreaded…that the threats she'd been receiving related to her relationship with Ethan Wynn. She'd bought into his mind games without even realizing how much her heart, her body and her job were being compromised. She should have seen the sickness in him. She should have warned someone about his obsessive behavior. She could have saved lives. She could have saved Lexi—the kind of criminalist and successful woman of the world she aspired to be—from being terrorized and nearly murdered. But she hadn't. She wasn't sure she could truly trust a man again. And she was damn sure that she couldn't completely trust herself anymore.

Instead of explaining any of that, she simply didn't answer the question directly. "I don't want to be the poster child for the crime lab. I just want to do my job and stay behind the scenes."

Lexi's nostrils flared as she calmed her flare of temper. "It's okay. I understand. But giving him a sound bite or two might get him off our backs for a while."

Reluctantly, Zoe nodded. Her boss was gently asking a favor of her. "The next time I get any kind of break on the case, I'll call Mr. Fletcher."

"Right after you tell me."

"Right."

Giving Zoe a knowing wink, Lexi circled around the end of the table to look at the information scrolling across her laptop. "Working on your dad's accident investigation, too? Have you connected a useful suspect to any of those prints yet?"

Zoe quickly pulled the oversized lab coat together in front of her and nodded. She'd been able to keep her secret for nearly six months now, but she wouldn't be able to for much longer.

"If I can find something useful, I'll turn the information over to the detectives working the case. No one around here likes a police officer being targeted. Even if Dad has been off the front lines for a few years now."

Lexi slid her arm around Zoe's shoulders and gave her a sideways hug. "And a loyal, loving daughter doesn't like anyone going after her daddy."

For a split second, Zoe leaned into the human contact that had been sorely lacking from her life recently. But before her actions revealed too much, like how desperately isolated she felt, she pulled away and nodded. "He's been my only parent for most of my life. I'd do anything for him."

"So would we." Lexi crossed her arms in front of her and transformed from almost a friend to Zoe's supervisor once more. "As long as you stay current with your regular assignments, keep working on finding out who caused Brian's accident. If you think you're onto something, let me know. I'll either assign someone to help you pursue the lead or I'll have them take over the rest of your caseload. Your father is like a dad to all of us around here. Any of us will help…if you ask."

"Thank you." Zoe meant that. She really would've liked to reach out to Lexi and her teammates for friendship and help. But showcasing that she had a new friend might just put Lexi on her stalker's radar, too. And she wouldn't allow that to happen. "Did you need something? Was this visit just about Jordan Fletcher? Or is the unnatural quiet around here getting to you, too?"

"Well, I have caught up on a ton of paperwork. But it's nice to talk to an actual, live person."

"Glad I fit the bill. You know, being alive and an actual person."

Lexi laughed. "You're funny, Zoe. I wish I knew you better."

The feeling was mutual. But until she could figure out the threats against her and could risk more, she'd settle for this quiet conversation and treasure the effort her supervisor was making.

"Um, there actually is a reason why I sought you out," Lexi said.

"Yeah?"

"I understand that you and my brother have become friends behind my back."

Any sense of calm immediately vanished as her nerves kicked in. "I wasn't trying to sneak around. It just happened. Then his leave was up and he went back to the Middle East, and then—"

"It's okay." Lexi rested her hand on Zoe's shoulder and smiled, as if Zoe and her brother being friends was a good thing. "You don't have to explain anything to me. I'm just glad Levi connected with you. For both your sakes. He's been all *oorah* and responsibility for far too long. He needs a woman and some gentleness in his life. And I know he's a nice guy."

"He is. But we're not—"

"He's talked to me about you a little bit," Lexi confessed.

Zoe wondered if the air conditioning had mysteriously kicked on or if she was generating her own chill. "He has? What did he say?"

"He was worried. Wanted to know if I could tell him anything."

"Oh. Um—"

"Maybe you could come over to the house tonight and show him yourself how you're getting along."

"Come over?" she echoed, fighting through her overwhelming embarrassment and regret to maintain a coherent thought.

"Aiden and I are throwing a little welcome-home party for Levi. He'll be in the Marine Corps Reserves for a couple more years, but he's officially not on active duty anymore. I just want to celebrate having him home in one piece."

"Is he okay? I know he got hurt."

"He says he's healing well. But he's got some nasty scars and some bad memories that seem to be impacting his sleep. And that lack of sleep seems to be affecting his moods... I'm sorry." She held her hands in an unnecessary apology and put on a brave face. "It was just him and me for a long time, so I can read him pretty well. He's trying to play the cool big brother, but something's eating at him."

Me! Zoe almost shouted. *The way I treated him is what's upsetting him!* "I would like to see for myself that he's okay." It was an honest wish, but she was already shaking her head. "But I'm not much of a party girl."

"It'll be a small gathering. I know you're not a fan of big crowds or the spotlight."

"You know about my anxiety?"

Lexi smiled. "I guessed. I admire that you don't let it affect your work, but I can see you struggling sometimes when you have to speak at one of the staff meetings or testify in court or get interviewed by a reporter."

Zoe nodded. "I have panic attacks when I get stuck inside my head and get overwhelmed. And if I have to—if my heart is racing or I can't breathe properly—I have meds I can take to make me zone out. But I try to cope with exercise, therapy and avoiding triggers when I can." Zoe shrugged. She didn't have to share her condition, but if Levi had been talking about her, he had probably already shared some of the eccentricities she had to deal with. "I suppose I do prefer a quiet evening to hanging out at a loud bar or a party. I can do it if I have to, but—"

"This will be a quiet evening," Lexi promised. "Well, except for having two working dogs and a fearless toddler in the same house." That kind of chaos sounded like Zoe's own family gatherings—and she'd handled those without many serious incidents until recently. "Aiden and I would love to have you join us. Levi will be the guest of honor, of course."

Two working dogs. "Sky is there, too?"

Lexi smiled. "You *do* know my big brother. Yes, Sky retired and came home with him."

A painful longing to see the man she'd fallen in love with that summer squeezed her heart. But she wasn't the same woman she'd been then, and he wasn't the same man. "I've been worried about Levi. I know he was hurt in an explosion. Is he truly all right?"

"He'll have some scars, and he's dealing with the emotional trauma. The young man who brought the bomb to the base was a local that he'd befriended."

"That's horrible." A friend had betrayed him? No wonder he'd practically gone ballistic when he'd accused her of betraying him, too. "Emotional trauma can be harder to get past than any physical injuries." She spoke from experience.

Lexi reached across the metal table to squeeze her hand. "You're always so insightful." She released Zoe's hand and put on a brave smile. "But he completed his tour of duty and is retiring after twenty years with the Corps. I've already made arrangements for him to visit a veterans' support group that meets at St. Luke's Hospital. They even let them bring their dogs if they have them. I have faith that the healing he needs will come."

"That's good. That's really good news." But for Levi's sake, for her own sake, she had to be honest. "I don't know if he'd want to see me, though. We had a fight the last time we talked. My fault."

"Trust me, Levi wants to see you."

Why? To lambaste her again for refusing to stay in touch the way she'd promised?

Lexi didn't push. "Think about it. I'd love to see you there. I'm sure Levi would, too." Pointing to the laptop in front of Zoe, Lexi abruptly changed the topic. "Are you having any luck identifying the fingerprints?"

Exhaling a sigh of relief, Zoe reached for the mouse. Work was a topic she could always talk about. "Dad's, of course. At least one other set of prints belongs to the mechanic who works on his truck." She pulled up a photo of the damaged truck. "But there are fingerprints down here at the bottom of the fender near the running board. Odd placement if you ask me."

Lexi flexed her fingers into the position of someone who would have grabbed the bottom of the truck. "As if someone held onto it there to slide beneath the truck and tamper with the brake lines?"

"There are other prints I haven't matched yet. But that's the one that concerns me."

Lexi nodded her approval. "Good catch. You can leave the program running after you leave, if you'd like, and still come by the welcome-home party. You don't have to bring anything. Just yourself. Levi is anxious to see you."

She wasn't so sure about that. "I'll think about it."

Lexi squeezed her hand again before heading to the door. "Don't work too late. You look like you need some rest and a good meal in you." She threw out her hands, as if she'd just had a eureka moment. "Hey, we'll have lots of food at the party. You can eat there."

Zoe summoned a genuine smile at the offer. "Thanks for thinking of me."

"Don't thank me. Just come."

Chapter Five

Nearly an hour later, Zoe drove by Lexi and Aiden's home and pulled into a parking spot across the street. She killed the engine and gripped the steering wheel tightly in her gloved hands as she turned her head to take in the scene.

There was still a decorated Christmas tree inside the front bay window. She recognized Aiden's Belgian Malinois, Blue, lying on the curved bench seat in the window, watching the world go by. A spotlight shone on the American flag flying from a porch pillar, and a banner that read *Welcome home, Levi!* was draped between that pillar and the one on the corner. There was a giant stuffed bone with a red bow tied around it and a tag bearing Sky's name leaning against the siding beside the front door. A circle of light from the nearby streetlamp illuminated most of the front yard. She smiled when she saw a big snowman. It wore a camouflage utility cap and a khaki scarf with a three-striped sergeant's patch pinned to its left side above its stick arm.

She'd just stop by for a few minutes—keep her bulky winter coat on and make an excuse to leave. She'd even lock her purse in the car, a sure indicator that she didn't intend to stay long. But she really wanted to see Levi with her own eyes, make sure he was still in one piece. And he'd promised she could meet Sky when he came home—she'd been looking forward to meeting the K-9 partner who was so important to him.

She could do this. She wanted to do this. Even if Levi was cross and didn't greet her with a big hug, Zoe needed to see him, thank him for his service and welcome him home. Inhaling deeply, she looked up and down the street, waiting for a car to drive past and disappear into the darkness before she headed across the slush and new snow.

But she hadn't taken a step when her phone buzzed in her pocket.

Her momentary burst of bravery and hopeful feelings vanished in a split second. She mentally braced herself before tugging off her gloves and reaching into her coat pocket to pull up the text message she was 99 percent certain she didn't want to read.

I told you to go straight home.

Zoe nearly dropped her phone into the snow. She whipped her head around, watching the car that had passed her reappear in the light from the streetlamp at the next intersection and turn. She looked back the other way. There were so many cars parked on the street, she couldn't clearly make out all of them. There were four, six, ten windows on this block alone with their blinds up and the curtains open where someone could've been watching her.

Her breathing became erratic. Why wouldn't *he* leave her alone?

She flinched when her phone rang in her hand. She wanted to hurl the hateful device away and disconnect from the entire world.

But she'd learned the hard way that if she didn't answer, *he'd* keep calling and calling. All through the night one time. Obviously, she hadn't slept. And when she'd staggered out the door the next morning to go to work, she'd found a letter on her car. The photo tucked inside was one of her at the park with her twin nieces. The threat inside had been simple and straight to the point.

Ignore me again, and I'll add these beautiful girls to my list.

They're in kindergarten in Warrensburg, right?

She hadn't ignored his calls again. She lifted her phone with a shaky hand and answered. "Hello?"

The mechanically distorted voice raked like claws against her ear. "Are you at a crime scene? Did I give you permission to go anywhere but straight home? Look what happened to your father when you didn't listen to me. Do you want something to happen to someone else? I want to see you at home. I'll be watching for you there. Disobey me, and I'll find the next thing on your list that you care about most, and I'll destroy it."

The silence of the disconnected call was deafening. She spun around in a full turn, expecting to see *him* watching her. Damn that tracking device anyway. She could remove it and give herself a respite from his daily pursuit, but then the messages would get more threatening. He might strike again.

Her gaze landed on the broad-shouldered man in the khaki sweater and blue jeans in Lexi's front window. Levi. His niece, Rose, sat in the curve of one arm as they both pointed to something on the tree.

I'll find the next thing on your list you care about most, and I'll destroy it.

He could've been watching Levi and his niece right now. He'd see how interested she was in the man with the military haircut and the pink, mottled scar tissue along the side of his neck. He'd target Levi or Lexi and Aiden or even little Rose if he found her watching the house, if he sensed how desperately she wanted to be a part of that world.

The puffy clouds of her breath in the cold air distorted her view and told her she was starting to hyperventilate. Not that she'd ever spotted the stalker himself. Sometimes she thought there was a familiar car... But she could barely see anything now.

Moving on instinct, she unlocked her SUV and climbed back in behind the wheel. She started the engine and cranked the heat before tossing the phone into her cup holder.

Zoe felt sick to her stomach as she pulled out onto the street. But she couldn't blame morning sickness this time. She'd made it through the next intersection when the whole center console vibrated with another incoming text. The message popped up on the screen on her dashboard.

Good girl.

"You son of a bitch." She swiped the tears from her eyes and counted her breaths—in through her nose and out through her mouth—willing herself to stay in the moment. God, she hated this. When would it end?

It was Ethan's controlling diatribe all over again. *Do what I say, and I'll love you. Disappoint me, and you'll regret it.* That whole train wreck of a relationship had been about pleasing Ethan, about unwittingly helping him retain his *normal* outward persona so that no one would suspect the evil he inflicted on innocent women. He'd called her weak, promised to protect her from the things that frightened her—so long as she showered him with affection and minded his every whim.

Zoe pounded her fist against the wheel and screamed. "It can't be you!"

And yet this was the same controlling nightmare. Was she so emotionally fractured that the crazies and stalkers of the world were the only men who wanted her?

At the next stop sign, she squeezed her eyes shut and willed the memory of Levi's deep, rumbly voice into her head, comforting her. Praising her. Telling her she was okay, that she was better than okay. Levi was a good man. *He* wanted her. At least, he had.

Maybe she was too broken to be happy—to deserve happiness.

She felt a small flutter of movement in her belly and instantly put her hand there. "*You're* not broken, sweetie. *You* deserve happiness."

As if sensing his mama had needed a little nudge to ignore the terrifying chaos inside her head, the baby shifted again—a soft swish of movement, like a wave gently lapping against the shore. "Don't worry, little one. I'll do whatever I have to in order to protect you. Mama will keep you safe."

The intimate conversation between mother and baby didn't completely push the panic away. But it was a reminder that she needed to stay in this moment and focus on getting them both safely home.

The twenty-minute drive passed like molasses in the cold evening, and Zoe was exhausted by the time she pulled into the parking lot of her apartment complex, parked in her space and got out of her car.

With her only goal to get inside her apartment where she could let go of the tight grip she had on her emotions and collapse beneath a warm blanket to succumb to her fatigue, she forced one foot in front of the other to get inside.

But she wasn't to be granted even that small boon.

"Zoe! Zoe, wait up!" Muffled footsteps hurried across the parking lot to catch up with her as her neighbor, Gus Packard, shouted her name. She quickened her pace and kept walking, knowing she was way beyond being "peopled out." He huffed up beside her before she reached the stairs leading up to her second-floor apartment. When he spun around in front of her, she stopped in her tracks so she wouldn't accidentally bump into him. "Hey, there, pretty lady."

"Hey, Gus." The young man was a few years younger than

her, with shaggy blond hair that brushed his shoulders and a gap between two of his front teeth where he often stuck a toothpick. She was pretty sure Gus had a crush on her. But since his cleanliness left something to be desired and his flirting style was like something from a middle school dance, the feelings were not returned. Good manners dictated that she be nice to him, but she didn't really want him hanging around. "How's it going?"

"Great. Hey. Cold enough for you?" Ah yes, the toothpick was firmly wedged between his teeth. The thing didn't even move when he spoke. He tugged nervously on the scarf his mother had knit for him. "Tomorrow is trash-pickup day. I was just taking Mom's and mine out to the dumpster. I can grab yours, too, if you want. That way you don't have to come back out in the snow. I can help you. Then you'll like me."

"I like you fine, Gus," she politely assured him. "But, um…" She didn't really relish the idea of coming back outside once she reached her apartment—not because of the winter weather, but because of *him*. "All right. That would be nice." He beamed all the way up the stairs and while he waited for her to unlock her door. "I'll be right back."

She barely pushed her way inside before she closed and locked the door behind her. She grabbed the trash from the bathroom and dumped it into the bag beneath the kitchen sink. Then she tied it off as she went back to the door.

Gus's gap-toothed smile had vanished as he hunched his shoulders against the cold, but he quickly smiled again as she handed him the bag. "Thanks again, Gus. This is awfully nice of you. Tell your mom hi from me. Good night."

"Bye, Zo—"

She closed the door and threw the dead bolt, then locked the knob and hooked the chain before hanging up her coat. She set her damp gloves on the small kitchen island to dry. Then Zoe circled through the apartment in her stockinged feet to check her window locks, close all of the blinds and make sure the curtains were drawn.

The gift *he* had given her taunted her from atop the desk in the small spare bedroom she'd set up as a home office. It was a stained-glass palm tree with a bright yellow sun peeking from behind its green leaves and a bikini-clad woman holding a can of beer and hugging the tree. Last night, she'd done some on-line research, trying to find where it had been produced and where *he* might have purchased it. It still sat in the clear evidence bag where she'd stowed it. Even if it hadn't come from *him*, it was the last piece of so-called art that would ever catch her eye. She wasn't a fun-in-the-sun kind of gal, she didn't like beer and she hated putting her body on display like that. Zoe paused for a moment, wondering if *he* knew how distasteful she found *his* gift to be. Maybe that was the point. *He* wanted to change her into *his* ideal of a woman. Something she could never be. Something she wouldn't do for any man again.

He wanted to see it on display in her window? "I don't think so."

Just when she was about to answer the rebellious urge to hurl the gift across the room and shatter it into a hundred pieces, a flash of movement beside the dumpster at the end of the parking lot caught her eye. Gus really was doing a nice thing for her, taking out her trash. She'd make a point to thank him again … "Ew."

Gus had opened her bag of trash and was rifling through it. She wasn't sure there was anything in there worth taking— torn-up junk mail, dirty tissues, spoiled leftovers and things she couldn't recycle. But that didn't deter his search.

"What the hell?" She quickly backed against the wall as he pulled something out and stuffed it into his coat pocket before glancing up at her window.

Had she made a mistake and thrown something personal away? Was there anything of value in there worth stealing?

Her paranoia nearly choked her. Surrendering to the idea that someone else—maybe everyone else—controlled her life now, she tore open the evidence bag and dutifully hung the ugly gift before pulling down the window shade and returning to the kitchen.

Knowing the baby needed sustenance even though she was too mentally exhausted to fix herself a meal, Zoe pulled a protein shake from the fridge and popped the tab. The sweet milky drink tasted like it was curdling on its way down to her stomach. But she forced herself to swallow it all before opening her bag and pulling out the evidence bag with the letter from this morning. She'd dusted it for prints and found none. Since it hadn't come through the mail, she couldn't trace its origin, either.

She'd lost count of all the letters and gifts she'd bagged these past months. But she was a trained criminalist, and the box of evidence bags stashed under her kitchen sink could add up to a circumstantial case against her stalker.

If she ever identified *him*.

If she survived his harassment campaign.

And she didn't lose her mind.

"Top-Top."

The tiny girl in Levi's arms said the same thing over and over again. She'd patted his cheeks, tried to climb over his shoulder, squealed with glee when he'd dipped her low, then swung her up in his arms. He wouldn't have thought his niece would have been old enough to remember Uncle Top from his last visit home, but apparently, Lexi and Aiden had talked about him often and kept his picture on the mantel. Or maybe she just associated him with the only word she knew because she'd been repeating "Top-Top" and reaching for him all evening.

The only time she'd paused was when he'd shown up with

Sky after he and Aiden had met at a nearby park to introduce their two dogs at a neutral location. Although the two K-9s had gotten along okay, they were clearly two alpha dogs and would have to be watched until they accepted each other as teammates.

He'd never been so relieved at how well Sky was trained when Rose shouted "Ky-Ky" and lurched toward the German shepherd. Especially since Blue was so protective of his human girl. Levi had quickly put Sky into a down-and-stay position while Aiden had hooked Blue to his leash and done the same. Seeing Blue lie down at Aiden's feet and Sky roll onto his side to allow the toddler to pet his tummy and neck assured him that they weren't about to have a violent confrontation. Still, he'd make sure that Sky was leashed or crated for the first few days when both dogs were in the house. He'd give him plenty of exercise. And Aiden had suggested they could do some training together at a facility called K-9 Ranch to further develop each dog's sense that they belonged to the same pack.

For now, Sky was resting comfortably in Levi's bedroom. The handful of friends who'd stopped by had already gone home. His stomach was full of the barbecue and side dishes Lexi had catered the party with, and Levi was on babysitting duty while Lexi and Aiden took a break from hosting and wrangling Rose.

At the Christmas tree, Rose reached for an ornament with his childhood school picture on it. "Top-Top."

"That's right. That's me. That's Uncle Top." He glanced over to Lexi and Aiden. "She's really smart to recognize me with braces and spiky hair."

Lexi smiled and leaned into the drape of Aiden's arm around her shoulders. "It's because I told her that was you when we hung it."

Aiden quickly disagreed. "No. It's because my daughter is brilliant."

Levi laughed. "Spoken like a proud papa."

"Just wait, bro. When you get a little one and she turns those big eyes on you and smiles, you'll realize you'd do anything to protect her. No matter what anyone else says, you'll think she's beautiful and smart and absolutely perfect."

Lexi nudged her husband playfully in the side. "Hey, that's what you said about me."

He leaned over and kissed her on the lips. "What can I say? I have a type."

Levi smiled. He'd known his best friend was in love with his little sister years before they'd married. But Aiden had been a foster sibling in their home, and he'd put his loyalty to the family who'd saved his life ahead of the desires in his heart. He only regretted that it had taken a serial killer targeting Lexi to make Aiden step up, to not only protect her but to love her as well.

Levi's chest expanded with a heavy sigh of envy. He thought he'd found the woman he would spend the rest of his life with this summer. But somehow his relationship with Zoe had tanked.

"Top-Top."

When he realized Rose was grasping for the ornament and pulling on a branch, Levi quickly shifted his attention. "Whoa, there, little one." He grabbed her tiny hands to keep her from tipping the tree over. As he turned her away, he looked through the window and saw someone he wasn't sure he'd ever see again.

"Zoe."

"Is she here?" Lexi popped up off the couch to join him at the window. "She was still at the lab when I left, working on her dad's case. She said she'd try to stop by."

Levi handed Rose off to Lexi and rushed to the door. "Zoe!"

But she'd gotten back into her car and was speeding away by the time he hit the edge of the front porch. "What the hell?"

Aiden followed Lexi and him out onto the porch. "Are you sure that was her?" he asked. "Could she have gotten called away on a case?"

"No," Lexi insisted. "I would have gotten the call first and then notified the team."

"That was her." Levi scrubbed his hand over the top of his hair and cursed. "She drives that silly pink SUV. It was parked across the street. She was outside of her car, but I saw her jump back in and drive away."

"Is she still not feeling well?" Aiden asked as they followed Levi back into the house. "You said she's been losing weight."

"Actually, I said she's swimming in her clothes. Like she can't find things that fit."

Ignoring the conversation, Levi marched straight to his room to grab his coat and keys. Sky stood up in his crate the moment he opened the door, whining with anticipation. Levi let him out and put Sky's harness around the dog's chest and shoulders. He pulled his black watch cap over his short hair, feeling the same readiness to take action the dog did. "Sky. Heel."

Lexi and Aiden were still talking about Zoe when they reached the front door. Lexi rocked a sleepy Rose in her arms. "Zoe has had a rough couple of months, and I don't know if she's getting the help she needs."

"*I've* had a rough couple of months," Levi said, reaching around her to open the door again. "She's avoiding me."

"She was brave enough to come here. That has to count for something." Lexi caught him by the arm before he stormed out. "Levi. Be gentle with her. She's more fragile than you know."

"I'm not going to hurt her, kiddo. I just need answers." He frowned at his sister. "Unless you know something."

"Not enough. I've reached out to her a few times, tried to

get her to open up. But that just seems to make her withdraw even more."

Levi nodded. That withdrawing was a sign that Zoe was trying to avoid having a panic attack.

"I know she's in some kind of trouble, but whatever it is that's making her look like death warmed over, you should hear it from her," Lexi said.

"Exactly." He leaned over to kiss the top of her head. "Thanks for the party and the Rosie-time. Love you."

"Call me later," she ordered, probably just as worried about Zoe as he was, although certainly not as angry.

Aiden put his arm around his girls as Levi headed out. "You need anything, you call me for backup."

"Roger that."

Chapter Six

Twenty-five minutes later, Levi pulled his truck into the parking lot of Zoe's apartment complex and pulled into a visitor's space. He hooked Sky up to his leash and got out. They jogged over to the dark pink SUV, where Levi took a quick walk around the vehicle. He didn't see any issues with the SUV itself, other than she'd left the door open over the gas port. So, no forgotten errand, no car trouble. She'd just wanted to get away from the Callahan-Murphy house as fast as possible.

Still, he wasn't going to let her run away from him and what they'd shared, and dump him without any kind of explanation. They'd been so good for each other. She'd told him she'd been happier, more grounded with him.

As his temper simmered back to the surface, Sky growled beside him, his posture straining forward. Levi knew what that meant. He whipped around, looking for the person who was foolish enough to try to sneak up behind him. A slightly pudgy blond man gave a startled yelp, then backed up several feet.

"Are you…?" His eyes were glued to the dog, although he was speaking to Levi. "Are you a friend of Zoe's?"

"Something like that." It wasn't much of an answer, but since he wasn't sure where he stood with Zoe yet, it would have to do. "Are you?" The young man's cheeks turned a ruddy shade. Was that embarrassment? Anger? "Levi Callahan," he offered when the other guy didn't answer.

"I'm Zoe's friend, too. I have to go." Then he turned tail and hurried up the stairs to the second-floor apartment directly across from Zoe's.

Levi dismissed the weird neighbor's hasty retreat. A lot of people were afraid of the muscular German shepherd at his side even before he went into battle mode. Reaching down, he patted the dog's flank and praised him. "Good boy, Sky. Way to have my back. Let's go."

Time to get this confrontation—er, conversation—over with. They jogged side by side up the steps to the second floor. Levi didn't like that she had an outside entry to her apartment. But Zoe had insisted this was a nice neighborhood and that her father had vetted the complex and checked the security himself before she moved in. At least she wasn't on the first floor.

Levi shook his head. Protection mode was his default setting and was a lot easier to deal with than ghosted-boyfriend mode. The first was stronger than the latter. He didn't like that he was a little nervous about how the face-to-face reunion would go. She was in the wrong. And he…missed her. He hated that she had that power over him when he was feeling so raw and distrustful inside.

He had to bury that needy weakness right now. He raised his fist and pounded on the door.

"Zoe! It's Levi. Let me in. We need to talk." When he didn't get any kind of response, he knocked again. "I thought we shared something special, Zo. Something that was going somewhere."

He paused with his fist in midair, ready to knock again when he heard a soft voice from the other side of the door. "We did. It was."

That was all he needed to hear. Something inside him softened at just hearing her voice. "Then please open the door." He was alarmed to hear just how many locks she disengaged on the other side. And was she sliding a chair away from the doorknob? "Zo?"

"Hey!" The screechy voice was accompanied by high heels tapping down the steps from the floor above him. A woman wearing a flowered silk robe over a matching nightgown with a pair of high-heeled slippers that had feathers over her toes stopped on the landing halfway above him. She wore gloves, but they were merely white cotton, not heavy enough to provide any warmth. His thought that the woman must've been freezing was cut short by her high-pitched haranguing. "Do you know what time of night it is, mister? Making all this racket? Some of us have to work in the morning." She clutched her robe together and started down the stairs in front of him. But she froze when Sky growled beside him, and she backed up a step. "Keep your wolf on a leash, okay?"

"Not a wolf—working dog. He'll do exactly what I tell him to."

Her bright red lips opened in a gasping O, as if he'd threatened her. "You're *making* him growl at me?"

No. He was just explaining. "Sky, sit."

The dog plopped down onto his haunches. Levi didn't have time for making nice. He needed to talk to Zoe.

But he had a feeling this neighbor had a flair for drama that would poke at his last nerve. The hour wasn't that late, and he was done being polite. "Zoe! I know you're there. Let me in."

The nosy neighbor pointed a long, white-gloved finger at him. "Do I need to call the police for harassing that sweet girl?"

"Lady, this is none—"

The door opened just enough for Zoe's face to appear in front of the shadows behind her. "No, Poppy, you don't. Thank you for looking out for me. But Levi is a friend." She dropped her voice to a whisper. "I hope."

The impact of her beautiful blue eyes stopped up his ability to speak for a moment. Her long, dark hair was pulled up into a messy bun on top of her head. But the shadows beneath those eyes and the pale cast to her skin made him long to pull her into his arms and shield her from whatever had stamped that weary expression on her face.

Zoe didn't open the door any farther, but she cleared her throat and spoke in a stronger voice. "Master Sergeant Levi Callahan, my upstairs neighbor Poppy Hunter. We look out for each other, water each other's plants, pick up each other's mail when I'm working a double shift or she's out of town visiting friends."

Introductions made, Poppy came down the stairs and joined him on the landing, her demeanor changing from nosy neighbor to openly flirting as she peeled off a glove and held out a hand manicured with deep red nail polish and adorned with at least one ring on all five fingers. "My skin is extra smooth tonight. I've been doing a treatment on them," she explained. "*Master* Sergeant, hmm?"

"US Marine Corps," Zoe added.

"Wanna feel?" the older woman offered.

Levi dutifully reached out to clasp just her fingers in his gloved hand.

"Oh. You can't feel my skin with your gloves on." Poppy practically pouted before clenching her hand around his, pulling herself close enough for him to smell the flowery perfume she wore and smiling, in full flirt mode. "I can tell he's a Marine." He arched a curious eyebrow at her assessment. "The posture? The muscles? I suppose you have a jarhead cut under that stocking cap. I bet you look as good out of uniform as you do in it."

"Poppy!" Zoe piped up, scolding her friend for hitting on him. "Don't you have a boyfriend?"

Poppy sighed. "A girl can still look and appreciate the scenery."

"Nice to meet you, ma'am." Levi pulled his hand away and pushed open the door. Zoe recoiled from his approach. "If you'll excuse us."

"'Ma'am'?" Poppy whined from behind him and pulled her glove back on. "Well, that sure popped the bubble on my fantasy."

He turned in the open doorway to find her standing with her hands on her hips and the top of her robe gaping open. "Ma'am, I don't want you to catch a cold."

She clutched her robe together and headed back to her apartment. "I'll let you two have your fun. Just keep it down. I need my beauty sleep. You be nice to my Zoe, hear me?"

"Yes, ma'am."

"Enough with the ma'am-ing already." She muttered something else Levi didn't catch before the door above them closed and locked.

He tugged on Sky's leash and stepped into Zoe's apartment.

She hugged her arms around herself and retreated from his advance. "I… I…didn't invite you in."

"You were fine with me being here this summer," he reasoned, hanging back near the door because he didn't like the way she was shying away from him. "I'm not going to hurt you. I just want to talk."

"It's not a good time."

"When *is* a good time?" Her gaze dropped to the middle of his chest and her nostrils flared with a ragged breath before she darted around him to lock the door. Just as he suspected, she had no answer for that.

"You have interesting neighbors." He tugged off his cap and gloves and stuffed them into his coat pockets.

Zoe paused in securing the locks behind him. "Neighbors? You met more than Poppy?"

He unzipped his coat. He nodded toward the windows over her couch, noting that shades were drawn and the drapes were closed. No wonder it was so dark in here. "Yeah. A guy from across the way approached when he saw me checking your car."

"Sounds like Gus. Gus Packard. Toothpick between his teeth?" Levi nodded. "I think he has a little crush on me." She went to the window and nudged aside the curtain to peer between the blinds without being seen. "He can see from his living room window into mine if I don't keep the drapes closed." The guy spied on her? "Why were you checking my car?"

Tracking your movements. Piecing together a reason for your abrupt departure without even saying hi. "You left the door to your gas tank open."

"But I didn't stop to get gas." Her delicate nostrils flared as she started breathing faster. She fiddled with the rolled-up sleeves of the faded black Missouri Tigers sweatshirt she wore. The shirt hung down to her hips, and the dull color made her fair skin look almost sickly. "Was there something wrong with it? Has it been vandalized?"

"Nothing I saw on a cursory glance." Her response made him think that something fairly disturbing was happening around Zoe.

She didn't elaborate. Instead, she offered him a weak smile and headed toward the kitchen. She turned on the light above the sink, but even that seemed to hurt her eyes. "May I get you something to drink? I don't have any alcohol, but I could make decaf coffee or some instant hot chocolate. A can of lemon-lime soda?"

Levi draped his coat over the back of the easy chair next to the couch and followed her. "Is this what we're going to do now that I'm home? Make polite chitchat until you can get me to leave?"

Frustratingly, she did exactly that. "I'm glad you're home safe. How is the healing going?" She glanced up at the mottled pink skin he knew showed above the collar of his sweater. "Are you still being treated for the burns?"

"Nope. No more sessions scraping off dead skin. Just getting used to the stiffness around all the scar tissue. There's a gel I rub in at night to help keep the skin supple. Got all my stitches out, too. Would you like to see my medical report?" he added with a touch a sarcasm.

"That sounds awful. I'm so sorry you were hurt like that."

He didn't miss that every time he moved, she turned to keep her back to him while she pulled out the fixings to fill her coffee maker.

Zoe finally gestured to the German shepherd sitting beside him, watching her jerky movements with curiosity. Sky was probably wondering what goodies she might pull out of the cabinets for him. For the first time since he'd shown up on her doorstep, she flashed a genuine smile. "Hey, Sky. It's nice to finally meet you in person." She glanced up without making it all the way to Levi's gaze. "May I pet him?"

"Sure. Sky, down." He unhooked the dog's leash, silently telling him he was off duty and could relax. Maybe having a buffer like Sky between them would make it easier for Zoe to talk. "He won't bite unless I tell him to. Or if someone threatens me."

Since Zoe had grown up around dogs, she knew to curl her hand into a fist and let Sky sniff her and okay her touch before reaching out to pet him. Sky must've been a sucker for her sweet vanilla scent, too, because he stretched his head up into her hand so she could better reach his favorite spots around his ears. "He's beautiful." She braced her other hand on the edge of the counter and awkwardly lowered herself to her knees beside the dog. She smoothed her hand along his back and flanks, inspecting the small reminders from the explosion. "Will the fur ever grow back over these scars?"

"No."

Zoe continued to pet the dog, taking the time to massage his shoulder joints. Sky's tongue lolled out the side of his mouth and he panted, enjoying his unexpected spa time. She changed her tone to something almost like baby talk. "The scars just add to your whole tough-guy persona. I bet nobody messes with you."

Wow. Levi was jealous of the damn dog. She was giving Sky the kind of tender attention he craved from her. That he *had* craved.

She gave the dog one more pat before she grabbed the counter again to pull herself up. "Should I get him a blanket to sleep on? Or a bowl of water?"

"If you want."

"I might have some dog treats left over from Christmas. I made a batch of peanut-butter-and-apple dog biscuits for Dad's Lab, Cody." Rising straight from her kneeling position, she stretched up to retrieve a sealed tub from the top of the refrigerator. But her fingers never touched the plastic. Her jeans slid off her hips and she jerked her hand down to grab the waistband. She tugged them back up, but not before he saw the glint of a giant safety pin holding the front of her unzipped jeans together.

Wait. Why were her pants riding so low on her hips? What the…? He reached for the hem of her sweatshirt and tugged it up to her waist to reveal the truth. "You're pregnant."

Zoe smacked his hand away and pulled the shirt down to hide her bulging belly. Without responding in any way to his discovery, she opened the tub of treats and fed one to Sky. Then she fixed him a bowl of water.

"How far along are you?" Her fingers trembled as she carried the coffee carafe to the sink to fill it with water. Still no answer. "Is it mine?"

The carafe clattered into the sink. "Yes, it's yours. You think I cheated on you?"

"I don't know. It would explain why you stopped communicating with me. You moved on. While the cat's away, the mouse will play."

"How dare you." Zoe was vibrating with nervous energy. She shut off the water and turned to face him. "You know how hard it is for me to be with people sometimes. You think I could handle more than one relationship? That I'd want to? Why are you being so mean? You need to leave." She pushed him toward the door.

He didn't budge. "Why didn't you tell me? I had a right to know I created a life with you. You couldn't have called me? 'Hey, Levi, I missed my time of the month, and the stick is blue.'"

"Don't say things like that." She quickly turned around, walking herself into a corner.

"You couldn't shoot me a text? Send me a damn postcard? Were you ever going to tell me?" He scrubbed his palm over the top of his hair. "Are you embarrassed to have my baby?"

"What? No." She yanked a towel from its hanging spot and wiped it across the edge of the sink and countertops where she'd splashed water from the coffee pot. "I tried to tell you I'm pregnant during one of our chats."

"You should have tried harder."

She twisted the damp towel in her hands, her knuckles turning white. "I said we needed to talk. But you were mad. And then you got hurt. You needed to focus on getting better."

Seemed he was always mad now. "How did this happen?"

"I told you I wasn't on birth control—I can't take the extra hormones in my body." She shrugged. "A condom must have failed. Or that one time when we got carried away and forgot and you pulled out—maybe it was already too late…"

"So, this is my fault?"

She tossed the towel at the sink as she darted past him into the living room. "It's no one's fault. You weren't the only one who wanted to make love. This isn't an accident I'm blaming you for. That's not why I was avoiding you… This baby is a blessing as far as I'm concerned. I'm trying to protect him… I can't have…certain people know. If they do, they'll hurt…" She was alternately running words together and gasping for air. Oh, hell. She was ratcheting up to a full-blown panic attack. "They already went after Dad. His T truck was sabotaged. I still don't have a sus-suspect. He could have died in that crash. I won't let them—"

"Zoe, calm down." It took him three long strides to reach her. He clasped her gently by the shoulders and turned her to face him. "You're not making sense. This can't be good for the baby."

She swatted his hands away and paced to the bedroom hallway and back. "I get my blood pressure checked regularly. And I have an ob-gyn. I'm doing my best, but I can't take the stupid anxiety meds at all now… Some are safe but may still have side effects on the baby…and I won't risk—"

"Zoe. Stop." Levi planted himself in her path and put his hands on her shoulders again, holding on as tightly as he dared. He hunched down to look her straight in her wild eyes. "You need to slow down your breathing. Come on, let's sit."

She jerked in his grasp, fighting off his touch. "No! You don't even want to be here. You're mad at me. I don't blame you. But…"

Enough. Levi dropped one arm behind her knees and scooped her up into his arms. She struggled weakly against him, but he carried her to the sofa and sat with her on his lap. Before she could move away, he wrapped her tightly in his arms and pulled her against his chest. "Shh, babe," he whispered softly, rocking her in his arms. "I'm sorry I'm yelling. I'm sorry I'm making it worse. I seem to have some anger issues, but that shouldn't matter. I'll try to control it better. You're all right. It'll be all right."

Her whole body shook and her hands fisted against him. "How can you say that? You don't even know—"

And then Levi did what he'd been aching to do for months. He kissed her. Gently, firmly, he pressed his lips against hers. He remembered how soft her mouth was, how sweet she tasted.

He knew the instant he'd broken through the haze of panic. Because after a shocked moment of being silenced, she responded. Her lips parted beneath his, eagerly accepting the solace he offered. One hand crept free of his grasp and curled up behind his neck to cradle the back of his head and hold his mouth against hers. He felt the pinch of her fingers on his skin as she fisted a handful of his sweater and T-shirt in her other hand. He breathed in the sweet vanilla scent of her lotion and savored the way her body clung to his. She surrendered. He took. She demanded, and he gave.

For a few precious seconds, everything righted in his world. The confusion, bitterness and blame vanished, and he felt a powerful sense of calm flow through him. The desire to deepen the kiss, to touch her body and reacquaint himself with the new curves he hadn't yet explored and the soft skin he remembered, to bury his fingers in that velvety waterfall of chocolate-brown hair to possess her mouth the way she already possessed his unwilling heart was like a hunger in him. Zoe Stockman was in his arms again.

But too much had happened these past few months for him to make himself completely vulnerable to his need for her.

He wasn't sure where he found the strength to end the kiss—probably when he felt the tremors of her fingertips against the back of his neck. —He gave her one last, chaste kiss, then tucked her forehead against the side of his neck. "That's it, babe. Take a time-out. Breathe with me." He splayed her hand in the center of his chest, covering it with his own. They both watched them move up and down with every deep breath he took. The close contact and practiced breathing seemed to take the edge off his anger and soothed her as well.

She pulled her knees up and curled into him as he pulled a pink blanket off the back of the couch and tucked it around her. He saw Sky watching them curiously from the edge of the kitchen and called him over. Levi patted the sofa cushion beside him. "Up."

The dog curled up on the seat next to Levi, his furry head resting on Levi's thigh, touching Zoe's hip. Good. Now she could feel cocooned by warmth from all sides.

Eventually Zoe's breathing slowed and synced with his. She stopped shaking and gradually gave him her weight.

They sat like that for nearly fifteen minutes before he felt her heavy sigh against his neck. "I've missed this. I've missed feeling safe."

Now those clues nudging at his subconscious started to gel into suspicion. But instead of pressing her for answers, Levi decided to take care of the baby first. That meant taking care of Zoe.

"When was the last time you ate?" he asked. "Lexi said you're losing weight."

"Actually, I'm gaining a little. I'm wearing bigger clothes to hide that I'm pregnant. I don't want anyone to find out. This is one of my brother Tyler's old college shirts." If she wanted to wear men's-sized shirts to cover her baby bump, he wished it was one of his. But if a big brother's shirt gave her comfort, then he wasn't going to bring it up. "I drank a protein shake when I got home. Sometimes it's hard for me to keep food down. I don't have much appetite."

That was her dinner? A protein shake? "And before that?"

She went quiet. Levi nodded, suspecting it wasn't recently and it wasn't as healthy or filling as it should have been. A plan was forming, but he needed to gather information first.

"Are you still having morning sickness?"

Zoe shook her head, strands of her hair falling from her bun and catching in the stubble of his beard. "I keep a couple of crackers on my bedside table and nibble on them in the morning. But it's not a big problem anymore."

"Anything make you queasy? Anything you crave?" This wasn't just practicality talking; he discovered he wanted to know these things about her pregnancy. About her baby. *Their* baby.

"I'm not a big fan of red meat right now. I'm craving salads, veggies, anything green. And I'd eat ice cream with just about every meal. But I have to make sure I don't gain too much weight."

It felt like she could do with a few extra pounds on her frame. "What time do you have to be at work tomorrow?"

"Um, ten? No staff meetings this week. But a few of us are managing the lab and answering calls. Unfortunately crime doesn't take a holiday."

He wasn't sure anything had been settled between them, but at least she was talking to him now. "You didn't take any time off for Christmas and New Year's?"

"I'm saving for my maternity leave."

"When's the baby due?"

"First week of April."

"And nothing you work with at the lab is a danger to the baby?"

She shook her head. "I talked to my doctor about it. As long as I follow regular protocols, there shouldn't be any dangerous exposure to anything. She said I could work right up until the baby comes." Zoe yawned for several seconds. "I may not want to be out in the field when my ankles and feet start to swell. Sitting will be much easier on my body than squatting or kneeling or standing."

Levi mentally filed away every piece of information to make sure she followed the doctor's instructions to the letter.

He'd run security procedures past Lexi, too, to find out how she'd handled working as a criminalist during her pregnancy. Only Lexi didn't seem to know that Zoe was pregnant. Would Zoe be upset if he shared her secret with people he trusted?

Her body grew heavier in his lap as weariness from what he suspected was much more than recovering from tonight's panic attack sucked the energy from her. He had a ton of questions— why no one knew about her pregnancy, why she wasn't wearing maternity clothes, why she wasn't eating well, why she kept her apartment so damn dark when he knew her to be a creature of the outdoors and fresh air and sunshine—and most of all, why she'd chosen to keep news of his child from him.

But every question could wait. Zoe was pregnant. She seemed so stressed that he doubted she was taking proper care of herself and the baby. If he was going to be a dad, he needed to be a father first. Then he could be a military cop and press for answers.

"All right. I want you to take a short nap. You okay if I leave Sky here with you?" She nodded. Levi got up, then laid her on the couch and tucked her in. Sky had merely scooted aside when he stood. Seemed his big, tough dog was already smitten with Zoe's massages, her praise and the homemade treats. He ruffled the dog's fur and silently approved of Sky's choice in women.

"I'll be gone thirty, forty-five minutes, tops. When I come back, I'll feed you, you'll get a good night's sleep. Then tomorrow morning, we'll have that talk."

"I've missed you, Levi," she whispered, already succumbing to her fatigue.

She had a funny way of showing it.

And what the hell was all that about feeling safe and keeping secrets and someone getting hurt?

"Wanted...make sure you're okay," she murmured drowsily. "Got hurt. Scared me. *He* made me stop. So sorry."

Levi tensed. Someone else had a hand in messing up the good thing they'd had going between them? "*He* who? What are you talking about?"

But sleep had already claimed her.

"I'll be back," he promised, grabbing his coat. He glanced at Sky, stretched out on the couch beside her. "Keep an eye on things."

Sky's dark eyes seemed to understand. He rested his head on the blanket but kept his gaze glued to the door as Levi pulled his watch cap over his head. Then he dug into Zoe's purse to grab her keys so he could lock the dead bolt behind him on his way out.

"Keep them both safe."

WELL, WELL, WELL. Wasn't this an interesting development?

The photographer snapped a picture of the pickup truck as it drove away.

Zoe Stockmann had a man friend. And not just anyone. A big, bruiser military hero, judging by the camouflage pattern and working-dog gear worn by the nasty-looking German shepherd with him.

That wasn't acceptable. She wasn't allowed to have anyone in her life except for the photographer. Pretty, pathetic Zoe wasn't supposed to think independently. She was supposed to be isolated, afraid, controlled.

But this man could throw a wrench into every detailed plan.

If the photographer couldn't get the job done, there would be no glorious victory, no recognition, no happily-ever-after.

First, Zoe flaunted the rules set up for her. When she fought back that first time, going after her dad had curbed that rebellious impulse.

Next, she couldn't find a damn clue to Emily Hartman's disappearance, even when the body had been moved to a more public location. Of course, the winter weather might have obscured Emily's resting place. After all, the weather was the one unpredictable factor in the long game the photographer was playing.

At least, it had been.

Now that man was in her life, at her apartment. It wasn't hard to verify that when she'd gone a different route after leaving the crime lab, she'd headed to his house. Was he an unpredictable factor, too?

Unacceptable. Completely unacceptable.

The photographer pulled out the last handwritten letter and read through it again, absorbing the glimmer of praise, the promise that the reward would be worth all this effort. "I won't fail," the photographer promised, renewed with hope.

It was all a matter of finding out more about the man with the dog and what they meant to Zoe—then severing that connection.

Zoe Stockmann belonged to the photographer. She was the puppet that would grant victory.

She was supposed to solve Emily's disappearance, raise a stir, get noticed, enjoy her fifteen minutes of fame. Then she'd be the next woman to go missing.

The rewards would be everything the photographer wanted.

Chapter Seven

28 December...

Zoe rolled over in bed and immediately had to pee.

Pressing her thighs together, she opened one eye, glanced over at the clock on her bedside table and sighed. "Come on, little one. My alarm hasn't even gone off yet."

She closed her eye and tried to get a few more minutes of rest. She was exhausted from the night before. A panic attack always left her feeling wrung out. But her exhaustion was more than that. For a few precious minutes last night, everything in her world had been normal and right. Levi had kissed her and held her and been the anchor she'd needed to reclaim control of her overstressed mind and body. She'd dared to feel hope and happiness again. That man wanting her, needing her, made her feel strong and capable.

But then he left. And the man who came back with sacks of groceries, a vanilla shake from a take-out restaurant and a bag from a discount store with two pairs of maternity jeans wasn't the Levi she'd known from last summer. He was all business. Maybe not angry like he'd been when he showed up at her door, but cold, detached—as if sharing those moments of closeness had upset him and he needed to distance himself from her now. He'd let Sky sit with her on the couch while he fixed her a huge salad and she sipped her milkshake. And yes, having the big, warm dog's head on her lap had been comforting, especially since Zoe wasn't sure what Levi was thinking.

But there'd been no more kisses, no more cuddles. Just a taciturn Marine doing his duty by a woman who needed his help. Then he'd announced he was camping out on her couch until they had the conversation she knew he deserved but she was dreading.

And that had set off as much emotional turmoil as him finding out about the baby.

Had Levi told anyone? His sister? His best friend? Did he understand just how dangerous it could be for his child if her pregnancy became public knowledge?

Had *he* seen Levi at her apartment? Followed him to the store and seen him in the maternity department?

Her poor brain, hardwired to overthink things, had come up with one horrible scenario after another about Levi getting hurt. He was built like the big, bad fighting machine he'd been trained to be. He was hyperaware and had a fierce K-9 partner by his side almost twenty-four seven. But that didn't mean he couldn't be taken out by a bullet or hit by a car on his morning run or poisoned. Oh, God—would *he* make his point by poisoning Sky? Losing his partner after working together for so long would devastate Levi.

And Zoe had already envisioned too many ways *he* could use the baby to hurt her. Cut him from her belly. Steal him from the hospital after he was born. Hold him hostage unless she did everything *he* said. She didn't even know what *he* wanted from her. He wanted to control her. He wanted her to suffer. He wanted to break her. But why?

It was Ethan Wynn all over again, and she had no idea how he was terrorizing her or what his endgame might be.

Only it couldn't be Ethan. Ethan Wynn was serving three life sentences and wasn't allowed to contact her or anyone else related to his trial. And yet someone was damn sure terrorizing her.

As a result, she'd had a lousy night's sleep, full of wishful dreams and familiar nightmares. But sleeping in this morning, or even sleeping till her alarm, wasn't an option. The baby wanted what he wanted, and sitting square on her bladder seemed to have become a hobby of his over the past month.

"Please?" she begged, cupping her hand around her belly. He answered by shifting inside her, and she felt a fusillade of flutters against her palm. Zoe smiled. "Good morning to you, too."

"Are you feeling all right?"

Startled by the deep-pitched voice from her doorway, Zoe bolted upright. With Sky standing by his side, Levi was still wearing the same clothes from last night, and he needed a shave. Yet his hair was damp, and he seemed fresher than she was feeling. "How long have you two been standing there? Did you shower?"

He thumbed over his shoulder to the hallway. "I borrowed your main bath—"

She held up a hand and scrambled to the edge of the bed, not really needing the answers to those questions at this moment. She dashed into the adjoining bathroom to take care of more pressing business. Levi was still filling her doorway after she'd washed her hands and come back out. Although Sky had decided to lie down and relax, Levi had a white-knuckled grip on the door frame, and his stony face was lined with concern. "Are you sure you're all right? Is the baby okay?"

Zoe sat on the edge of the bed and picked up a soda cracker to nibble on. "Sorry. My bladder is not my own these days. It's annoying, but I'm okay. We're both fine."

Levi hung back in the doorway, maybe remembering the nights they spent together here. Maybe leery about hurting her or saying the wrong thing. Zoe hated this awkwardness between them and realized it was up to her to move them past it. She polished off the cracker and washed it down with water from the bottle on her bedside table before waving Levi into the room. "The baby's moving this morning. It's not a kick yet, but he squirms around and makes himself comfortable, no matter what I need. It's more like whooshes or the last few pops of a firework right now. Would you like to feel him? Maybe her? I told the doctor I didn't want to know the gender. But I kind of feel like it's a boy."

"A boy?"

"Nothing scientific. Just a feeling. I'd be just as happy with a girl, as long as he or she is healthy."

Levi nodded and sat on the bed, though not close to her. Sky lay down at his feet. "What do I do?"

"Give me your hand." He placed his big, calloused palm in hers, but she hesitated. "Are you comfortable touching me?"

"It's not sexual." That was a little cold but nothing she didn't deserve. "It can't be. I'm not ready to be that open with you again. But I would like to meet my son or daughter."

Understanding the rules he'd put up to protect himself, even if she felt a stab of guilt at knowing her behavior was the reason he *needed* to protect himself, she lifted the long flannel shirt she slept in and placed his hand on her belly, moving it to where she felt the flutters. "He's starting to settle down, but—"

"I feel it. Him. Her. Like tremors." Levi moved his hand across her belly, following the movement. As he leaned in front of her, she inhaled him. He smelled of her own vanilla bodywash and the heated masculine scent that was uniquely him. Oh, how she missed this good man. And for the umpteenth time, she wished she'd met him before she ever knew Ethan and her world had been turned inside out. Her life could have been so different.

The intimate moment ended when Levi pulled away. "It's gone."

Zoe had to take another drink before she could find her voice again. "He's found a comfy place where he wants to sleep, I suppose."

With a curt nod, Levi stood and strode toward the door. Sky fell into step beside him. "Shower and get dressed, or whatever you need to do. I've got breakfast waiting for you in the kitchen."

Twenty minutes later, she walked into the kitchen, drawn to the smells of coffee and whatever yummy things were roasting in the oven. "Smells good."

"More of your brother's clothes?" he asked, serving up food he'd been keeping warm in the oven.

"They're warm. They hide my shape." She heated up some water in the microwave, made herself a cup of green tea and carried it to the table. "Besides, I'll either be wearing my lab coat or my winter coat over them, so no one will see that it's not the most professional outfit anyway."

"Can't you afford maternity clothes?"

"I can." She ducked her head to sip her tea. What she couldn't afford was *him* seeing that she was pregnant. *He* always seemed to know what she was doing, so even shopping online and risking *him* seeing a package on her doorstep or arriving at work would draw attention she didn't want.

"I thought expecting women liked showing off their extra curves. My sister wore some form-fitting stuff."

Zoe didn't answer the unspoken question. Instead, she brushed her hands over the stretchy denim on her thighs. "Thank you for the jeans. Now I won't worry about losing my pants if I move around too much."

He looked like he wanted to push the point, maybe offer to take her shopping or sit her down in front of her computer to order things online. Instead, he gave her a curt nod, accepting her thanks. "I roasted up a ton of veggies you can eat for a couple of days. I put some of them and cheese in the eggs I scrambled for you. Toast will be up in a sec."

"I knew something smelled wonderful." He buttered the toast, added it to the plate and set it on the place mat in front of her at the end of the table. "Are you planning to feed me three meals a day until I have this baby?"

"If I have to. Your health is critical to the baby's health."

Her enthusiasm for the delicious breakfast waned at the subtle reminder he was taking care of the baby and that the only reason she was benefiting from his generosity was because the two of them were connected. Levi stepped away from the table to refill his mug of coffee and grab a manila envelope off the island.

"Have you already eaten?" she asked, forcing down another mouthful of the cheesy eggs. He rejoined her at the table, laying the envelope in front of her. "What's all this?"

"I borrowed your computer last night. Printed off some forms." He swallowed a drink of coffee and set it down before pulling out several official-looking papers. "I have some things I'll need you and your doctor's office to fill out."

"What things?" She wasn't liking the sound of this.

"Insurance forms. I'm putting you on my TRICARE plan."

She set down her fork and cradled her mug of tea in both hands to try to dispel the authoritative chill Master Sergeant Bossy Boots was giving off. "I have insurance. I have a job. I'm already paying for my doctor. I don't want to switch to someone new."

He nodded. "We'll make that work, then. But this is my baby, too. I intend to support him or her. And help take care of you so they're healthy."

She appreciated his overdeveloped sense of responsibility, but there were some basic logistics here he was overlooking. "How can I be on your insurance anyway?"

Those green eyes bored straight into hers. "You and I are

getting married as soon as I can arrange it. Today, if possible. Tomorrow, for sure."

She replayed the words in her head to make sure she'd heard him right. "What?"

"I know what it's like not to have a mother and father. This kid won't."

"You think I can't take care of our baby?" She pushed her chair back from the table, really wanting to distance herself from Levi right now. "Because you think I'm a mental case?"

"I didn't say that. I never would. You're one of the strongest women I know, coping with everything you've had to deal with. But I'm not risking this child for any reason. Let me help." If only he knew just how much danger the baby might be in if they celebrated and broadcast his existence.

"I love this baby. So much. I would never put him at risk." She tried to explain some part of the nightmare she'd been living with. "That's why I've cut off ties to everyone—"

"You keep saying *him*. You have that strong a feeling that we're having a son?"

That wasn't the point she was making. Her hands slipped down to cradle her belly. "I don't know." Maybe she'd done too good a job of pushing Levi away. As the father, he did have rights she had no intention of denying him. "If you want to find out, you can come to my next ultrasound."

"I *will* come. He's been growing for six months already, and I never knew he existed until last night. I've never felt him until this morning." His eyes softened as he splayed his fingers and looked at his hand. But then he curled them into a fist that rested on top of the papers he'd given her. "That's going to change. My child is going to know me."

She nodded. "If you see anything in the ultrasound, you won't tell me, will you? I don't want to know. The anticipation of planning for a specific gender makes me a little nervous. What if I make a mistake and paint his room with blue trucks and it turns out to be a girl? Or vice versa? I was thinking of going with baby animals or maybe a dinosaur theme for the nursery . I was fascinated by them growing up." She dared to reach out and rest her fingertips lightly atop his fist, wanting to calm the tension radiating off him. "I just want to be ready to welcome this little one into the world and accept him or her, no matter what."

"I agree with that philosophy. And I like the animal idea." He glanced over at Sky, napping on the rug in front of the couch. "There are going to be dogs around, so he or she might as well get used to them." He relaxed his hand and turned it to clasp their fingers together. "Who's gone with you to the doctor before?" When she started to pull away, he tightened his grasp. "You've gone on your own?"

"Yes."

"Who's your coach in birthing class? Because they're being replaced now that I'm stateside."

She shook her head. "I haven't started a class yet."

Again, silence. He squeezed her hand, showing her a glimpse of the patient, compassionate man she'd fallen in love with. "You can't do all this by yourself."

Zoe pulled her hand away and picked up her plate. *Alone* was the safest way to be right now. "I can if I have to." She stood and carried her unfinished breakfast to the kitchen sink.

Levi followed behind her. "But you don't have to. I'm here now."

"Levi—"

"What's your work schedule like this week?" He leaned his hip against the counter beside her and softened his tone. "I'd like to be married before the end of the year. Justice of the peace work for you?"

"You're just going to announce that to me? Make all the decisions now?" She tilted her face up to his. "You're not going to *ask* me to marry you?"

"If there's any chance you might say no, then no."

Zoe's heart thudded in her chest. She went back to scraping the plates and loading the dishwasher, needing to keep her focus outward to stave off the sadness consuming her. "This is sudden. You know I need time to process things. I have to do what's right."

"What's right?" he mocked. He reached into the front pocket of his jeans and dug out a small, cube-shaped jewelry box. "I believed we were so right for each other that I bought a ring back in August."

Stunned by that revelation, she closed the dishwasher and faced him again. "You have a ring?"

"It was going to be my Christmas present to you. I was going to ask when my stint was up with the Corps." He snorted a laugh that held no humor at all. "But things changed. I was confused and hurt and angry, and I didn't know why. I stuffed it into the bottom of my duffel bag and tried to forget about it. But I figure it will come in handy now." He tossed her the ring box. "Marry me. For the baby."

Zoe caught the ring box and cradled it between her hands, not really wanting to open it under these conditions. She might actually have said yes if it hadn't sounded like such a cold-hearted business proposition. Deep down, she knew she loved this man. And she suspected he had once loved her. But that love could get him hurt. In a way, it already had. That love would be a thing *he* wouldn't hesitate to use against her.

The baby squirmed inside her belly, as if urging her to make the right decision for him. Her hand instantly dropped to caress the small life stirring inside her. Then she squeezed the ring box in her other hand and inhaled a deep breath.

She was going to say yes, because it was the right thing to do, the practical thing. For the baby. Having a military cop with twenty years of experience in the United States Marine Corps could be what she needed to keep the baby safe from *him*. Levi didn't love her anymore. But he would do everything he deemed necessary to protect the welfare of his child.

So, Zoe tipped her gaze to Levi's and nodded. Her voice was flat, but she didn't hesitate to agree to his proposition. "I'm on the day shift until New Year's Eve. Then I have three days off." The scowl on his face made her think he didn't like that answer. "But I get an hour lunch every day. Is that enough time to go down to the courthouse and take care of it?"

"Should be. I'll get the paperwork started today." He seemed surprised by her response, that she hadn't tried to argue her way out of the marriage. He propped his hands at his waist and nodded, then started talking as if she'd agreed to accompany him on some kind of military mission. "We'll need witnesses there. I prefer to have somebody we know. Lexi and Aiden okay with you?"

She nodded. "Can I ask my dad to be there, too?"

"Of course." Levi muttered a curse. "I know it's not the wedding of your dreams—of anybody's dreams—but I think it's important we get it done as soon as possible. For the baby."

"For the baby," she echoed.

"As soon as it's official, I'll put your name on my life insurance form, and we can decide how you want to handle your health insurance options."

She nodded again. "For the baby."

"I don't have my own place. I've been overseas more than I've been stateside for the past twenty years. But we can start looking—"

"We can live here in my apartment." If he was going to be so ruthlessly practical, then so could she. "There are three bedrooms. I use one for my office and one for storage. I was going to move my desk into the storage room and turn the small one into a nursery, but you can put a bed in there and use it if you'd like. There's room for a crib in my bedroom if we rearrange things."

Levi agreed with her suggestion. "Eventually, we'll look for someplace new. Bigger. He'll need a yard to play in, a room of his own. For now, this will do. I'm not thrilled with your neighbors, but I already familiarized myself with the layout of the complex on my morning run. I've gotten Sky acquainted with the scents he needs to be familiar with."

Her heart was breaking at how clinical he made the proposal sound—as if they were discussing a business deal and not a commitment to someone he loved. But she could put up with his distrust and accept an empty marriage. "For the baby."

"Now, I think we have another problem." He reached into his other front pocket and pulled out a black, coin-sized device and set it on the counter in front of her.

Zoe jumped back from the familiar tracking device. "Where did you get that?"

"From the gas port of your SUV. I looked at it again this morning. I'm guessing that's why the door was open."

"No. It was under the front left wheel well..." She snatched it up and hurried to the front door. "He'll think I removed another one and he'll—"

"Zoe, stop." A large hand folded around her upper arm and pulled her to a halt. "You don't even have on a coat or snow boots."

"I have to put it back." Frozen wet feet were hardly a deterrent to keeping *him* from making her life hellish again. "That's why he went after Dad. He'll hurt someone else if he finds out."

"What are you talking about?" He turned her slightly to grasp her shoulders between both hands. His green eyes reflected confusion as well as concern and even something a little predatory. "Tell me what's really going on. There seems to be a lot I don't know."

That predatory gleam was what she responded to. She returned to the kitchen, pulling out the box full of evidence and carrying it to the table. Levi came up beside her as she laid out all of the labeled evidence bags across the table. "If I'm going to marry you, then you need to know everything. Why I'm so scared. Why I'm hiding my pregnancy. Why I tried to let you go." She glanced up to find him scowling as he surveyed each piece of documentation. "Yeah. That look right there is what I need. I'm going to need you and Sky to do your scary Marine thing and help me do whatever is necessary to keep our baby safe."

He'd started thumbing through the bags until she'd said that. "Someone threatened the baby?"

"Not yet. But I think it's only a matter of time."

Levi sank into the nearest chair and picked up three of the letters she'd received. He frowned after reading the first one, cursed after the second, tossed them back onto the table as if they burned his hand after the third. "These are all addressed to you. Shouldn't they be at the crime lab?"

"It's not an official case."

"You haven't told the police?"

"At first, I dismissed it—as a practical joke or the perp left the letter on the wrong car. I thought maybe my anxiety was turning nothing into a big, scary something." She wrapped her arms around herself, desperately needing a hug. "But then I realized it was all deliberate. It's a lot like my relationship with Ethan Wynn. When I didn't do what he wanted, he threatened me. Left bruises on me more than once. The day he slapped me woke me up. I should have warned Lexi about the kind of Jekyll-and-Hyde guy he was, but—"

"Don't worry about Lexi. She's got Aiden with her now. They put Ethan away."

"With my help." He nodded, possibly remembering details she and his sister had shared about the trial. "At first, I thought this was retribution for testifying against him. I superimposed my issues with that relationship onto all this. I made sure Ethan was still in prison." She gestured to the pile of evidence bags. "But it didn't stop. When I tried to handle it myself, when I took that first tracker I found off the car—that's when Dad lost control of his truck and crashed. *He* warned me I shouldn't disobey *him* again."

"That wasn't an accident?"

She shook her head. "I examined the wreck myself. Had one of my coworkers confirm my findings. There were holes punched into the brake lines."

"Is this why you ghosted me?" He eyed each bag with the sharp eye of a military cop. "Did he threaten me in one of these letters?"

"Not specifically. But *he* called me in that horrible, distorted mechanical voice and said going after Dad was just a warning, that *he'd* hurt anyone I cared about if I didn't follow *his* instructions to the letter."

"You said *he*. But I don't see a name on any of this."

She hugged herself again and shook her head. "That's how I refer to *him*. In my mind, it's always in italics. I wish I had a name."

"What is it *he* wants you to do?"

"Suffer. Have a nervous breakdown. I'm not sure, but I think I'm being set up to do *his* bidding or pay a price—recant my testimony on an old case, lose evidence that could implicate *him* or someone important to *him*, solve a cold case for *him*, maybe even help *him* commit a crime, kill myself, I don't know." She shrugged, wishing she had the answer. "It's like he gets off on controlling me. Like I'm his puppet. Maybe it's just how that sicko gets his jollies, and he saw me as an easy mark."

The old Levi would have taken her into his arms by now. Tears stung her eyes when she saw his hands fisting down at his sides, as if he was forcing himself not to touch her. "And you haven't told anyone this?"

She wiped away the tears before they could fall. "I don't want anyone else to get hurt."

"He's hurting *you*."

"Tell me something I don't know." Zoe picked up her notebook from the table. It was heavier than she wanted to admit. "I started documenting everything. Creating a habitual trail of evidence. Like we do with a real stalking case."

"This is real, Zo. You're a victim like any of those other people you've helped." She opened the notebook in front of him. But Levi took over, skimming through the pages and shaking his head at the sheer volume of documentation.

"If he finds out about the baby...and I can't keep it hidden much longer—you figured it out within minutes of seeing me again...*he* won't hesitate to threaten him, too. *He* probably already knows that you spent the night and is plotting something to punish me for that." Zoe touched his shoulder again, needing him to look at her and see the sincerity of the deal she was making with him. "Can you help me keep the baby safe? If I marry you, will you protect us?"

Ironically, the grim look on his face gave her hope. He gave her a curt nod, then turned to a fresh page, pulled out a pen and started writing. "Tell me everything."

Chapter Eight

Levi bundled up and headed outside with Sky to replace the tracker he'd found on Zoe's SUV.

Zoe's reaction to seeing it had raised every protective hackle on the back of Levi's neck—figuratively, of course, since the burn scars had taken out the nerves there. The detailed box of evidence she'd gone through with him revealed the staggering weight of emotional turmoil she'd been dealing with while he was deployed.

It hurt that she hadn't confided in him sooner. He could have advised her, comforted her, put her in contact with people who could help her. At the very least, he wouldn't have let his feelings for her fester into the angry, distrustful knot of hurt and resentment that now blackened his heart. He wouldn't have lost months of knowing he was going to be a father.

He now understood that Zoe had distanced herself to protect him, irrationally thinking this creep would be able to hurt him from nine thousand miles away. He even understood keeping her pregnancy a secret. She'd been protecting their baby the only way she knew how—by not letting anyone know besides her doctor of his or her existence.

But Zoe's spirit was dying, keeping herself locked away from the world and setting aside relationships and support and any joy she might share over her pregnancy.

That sick game stopped today.

Levi knew how to run a protection detail. He might not have had jurisdiction outside of the military, but he would be the boots on the ground. And he had plenty of crime-lab and police connections. He'd call in favors. With Zoe's permission, he'd already called his sister and Aiden and set up a meeting for later this morning. All of Zoe's meticulous documentation would be turned over to the crime lab. He was going to find this guy and hand him over to his brother-in-law or her dad at KCPD. Zoe already had unusual stressors to manage with her anxiety issues. He was determined that she have a safe, healthy pregnancy and deliver his child without fear.

His troubled sigh created a cloud in the cold air. He opened the door to the gas port and quickly stuck the magnetic tracker back where he'd discovered it. Understanding *why* his young friend Ahmad had tried to blow him up and *why* Zoe had ghosted him did little to ease the shock and pain that he'd suffered.

He could do his duty by Zoe and the baby. He could keep them safe. But could he truly love and trust anyone again?

He let the tiny door slam shut and turned his head to find Sky following the scent of something he deemed of interest across the snow-packed parking lot. "Whatcha got there, boy?" Levi doubted he was on the trail of any kind of explosive in the suburban apartment complex. But he also knew the German shepherd could sniff out a candy bar in someone's pocket or the remnants of a fast-food sack in a trash can. He pulled Sky's leash from his back pocket and headed after him. "I already fed you eggs this morning, you spoiled rotten..."

Levi caught two small circular reflections in the second-floor apartment window a split second before the blinds came down and the shadowy figure he'd seen there disappeared. He didn't even take time to register the warning instincts surging through his blood. He glanced back up at Zoe's windows to see her opening the blinds and curtains in her living room.

Levi cursed and jogged after Sky. The dog wasn't tracking food. He was on the scent of someone that had been beside Zoe's car. And Levi knew who. They skidded to a halt on the landing outside the second-floor apartment. Sky danced beside him, panting with excitement over whatever find-the-prize or take-down-the-perp game he thought they were about to play.

Levi pounded on the door. "Open up!" What had Zoe said her neighbor's name was? Patton… Paxton… "Packard! I'm your new neighbor across the way. We have something we need to discuss. Open up!"

He heard a scuffle of movement inside and almost raised his boot to kick in the door to stop him from hiding or throwing away any kind of evidence. But he didn't have jurisdiction here, and there was no way to protect Zoe and the baby from inside a jail cell. He glanced down at Sky, knowing how to get the young man moving. "Sky. Speak!"

Levi repeated the command twice more. Sky's booming bark had a way of getting people to move faster and cooperate with Levi's orders. "Packard! We need to talk."

Almost instantly, he heard the click of the dead bolt unlocking. "Um…hi. Does your dog…?"

When the door opened slightly, Levi pushed his way inside, knocking the young man back several steps. The toothpick that had been stuck between his teeth fell to the floor. Levi didn't even cringe as the twentysomething picked it up and clamped it back inside his mouth. Instead, he crossed straight to the table in front of the window. He already knew that Sky would be taking up position behind him, keeping his eyes on the other man, who closed the door and nervously crept around the edge of the room, staying close to the wall where a giant TV set hung.

"You shouldn't be here," Packard whispered, sliding behind the sofa as if that would stop Sky from reaching him if Levi gave the command. "It's time for Zoe to go to work," he said, his eyes focused on the window instead of Levi and Sky. "Why isn't she going to work? Is she sick?"

Although there might've been something a little childlike about Gus Packard, he was still a full-grown man, and he'd just confirmed that he'd been spying on Zoe. The binoculars, camera, long-distance photographs of Zoe—both outside her building and shadowy images taken through her windows while she was inside—a paper coffee cup with a familiar print of orchid-pink lip gloss around the drinking spout on the lid and a weathered package addressed to Zoe told a disturbing story. "What the hell are you doing here? Spying on Zoe like some kind of perv?"

"Zoe's my friend," Packard answered, his gaze flashing from the window to Sky to the door and back to Levi. "Mom says I can't have friends here when she's at work. You have to go."

"I'm not your friend." Wait. Mom? This guy lived with his mother? "How old are you?"

"Twenty."

A familiar compassion he'd once felt toward Ahmad El Khoury tried to resurrect itself. But he squashed it down. There was still something very wrong going on here. For all he knew, Gus Packard could be a really good actor. And he wouldn't have to be a rocket scientist to be able to terrorize an innocent victim. Levi gathered up the photographs and stuffed them inside his coat, leaving his gloves on so that he wouldn't get fingerprints on them.

"Hey. Those are Zoe's things." Gus inched around the end of the couch.

"Exactly. You can't have this stuff. And pictures?" Levi's

hard gaze moved the young man back behind the furniture. "Do you understand how creepy this is?"

"None of my pictures are naughty," Gus protested. "I watched her putting on her pajamas once. But I didn't take a picture. That would be naughty. I found her cup in the trash. And the other was buried in the snow outside her door for two days. She didn't want it."

"She probably didn't know it was there. Stealing mail is against the law."

"But she didn't want it," Gus echoed softly.

As much as he wanted to teach this guy a lesson about spying on his woman, he doubted the young man would understand why it was so offensive. He eyed Gus's laptop. It was closed and off right now, but were there more pictures stored there? Copies of the typed letters she'd received? At least Levi could confirm that Zoe's paranoia about being watched wasn't unfounded. "They're an invasion of privacy. Zoe has the right to feel safe in her own home. Spying on her like this upsets her."

"It does?" The young man sounded confused.

Levi looked him straight in the eye and explained it as succinctly as he could. "When someone is watching her and she can't see him, she doesn't feel safe."

Gus's face was flushed, and he was breathing harder. "I don't mean anything by it. She's pretty and nice to me, and I like her. Zoe's my friend."

"Do you want to be more than friends?" he challenged.

The younger man didn't seem to grasp the question. "If you want to know who's spying on her, you ought to talk to that gray-haired guy with the noisy car who waits in the parking lot and takes pictures of her sometimes."

"What guy?" Damn. How many potential enemies did Zoe have around her?

"I don't know his name. He comes by on Wednesdays and Fridays. Parks and sits in his car, sometimes as long as two hours in the cold, waiting for her to come home."

"He takes pictures of her?"

Gus nodded. "He watches. Takes pictures. Then, when she goes inside, he calls someone on his phone and drives away."

Levi pulled the blinds aside to look down in the parking lot. He didn't see anyone sitting in their car right now. Then again, Wednesday was the day after tomorrow. If Gus was right, he wouldn't be here today. Levi wondered if he could convince Aiden to run names on every plate number in the lot, or get a list of tenants and find out which cars didn't belong. "You don't happen to have pictures of that guy or his car, do you?"

"Uh-uh. I don't like him. He yelled at me when I told him he was supposed to park in the visitor's space."

While Levi speculated on his next move, Gus came around the end of the couch again. Sky growled as he moved closer, and the young man stopped in his tracks. "Is your dog going to bite me?"

Levi patted Sky's flank, urging the dog to sit. "Not unless you attack me first or I tell him to."

"I wouldn't do that. I would never do that." Gus gave off the vibe of a cockroach, clinging to the shadows, happy to do his dirty things without coming out into the light to risk an actual confrontation. Although he was technically stalking Zoe, Gus couldn't be the man terrorizing her, could he?

Then again, Levi had never suspected that Ahmad El Khoury would turn on him and try to kill him, either.

"Can I take a picture of your dog? And pet him?"

Seriously? Could he really be that good of an actor to pull off sounding so guileless? "Not today." Levi had too much tension roiling through him, and he knew his emotions traveled down the leash to Sky. If he still didn't trust this guy, then the dog wouldn't, either. "Maybe another time."

Gus picked nervously at his fingernails. "Okay."

"That was good to ask, though." Levi felt enough pull toward this guy's childlike ways that he couldn't be a complete bully to him. "Not every dog is friendly, and if you stick your hand in the face of one you don't know, he might bite you."

"Does it hurt?"

"If he bites you? Yeah. Sky's not trained to be gentle." If he'd be more cautious about harassing Zoe because he was worried about Sky's teeth, that was okay with Levi. "Give me your cell phone. Unlock it for me."

Gus pulled his phone from his jeans, typed in his code and handed it over. Levi typed in his name and number. "That's me, Levi Callahan." Then he handed it back and waited for Gus's blue eyes to focus on him.

"Now, listen carefully. One, Zoe's taken. She's going to marry me. She might be your friend, but she will never be anything more. Two, you're giving me these pictures and anything else you've taken from her. And three, the next time you see that guy spying on Zoe, you're going to call me. You're going to take a picture of his car, write down his license-plate number and then tell me he's here. Can you remember that?" Gus had counted each point off on his fingers, carefully processing everything Levi said. He nodded. "Call me first. And don't approach this guy. He may be dangerous. I'll handle that. I just need you to tell me if he comes back here. Understand?"

Gus nodded again and sort of smiled. "I'd be helping Zoe? I'd be taking care of her? She wouldn't be upset with me, then, right?"

"You'd be helping Zoe stay safe." Levi held up a warning finger. "But if I see you looking out your window with those binoculars again, trying to get a glimpse of her in her apartment… Sky and I will come back to pay you another visit. And it won't be as friendly as this one."

Gus frowned. "This was friendly?"

Levi leaned in ever so slightly. "You don't want to see me *un*friendly."

Gus dashed around Levi and Sky. "She can have her stuff back." He grabbed a plastic bag from the kitchen and stuffed the weathered package and the paper coffee cup inside before handing it to Levi. Then he ran to the door and opened it. "I'll do it. I'll help Zoe. If I see that guy, I'll write down the number on his car, take his picture and call you. Zoe will be happy."

"Thank you, Gus." Levi toned down the intimidation factor another notch and extended his hand. If his grip was a little firm, the younger man didn't seem to mind. "You and I might get along after all."

Gus Packard now seemed eager to please him. "Then you'd be my friend? Sky, too? I could pet him if he was my friend."

Levi wasn't sure he'd go that far. But if the guy stopped spying on Zoe and agreed to put his voyeurism to a better use, he at least vowed not to break down Gus's door again. "We'll see." He tapped his thigh. "Sky. With me."

"Bye, Levi Callahan! Bye, Sky!" The young man laughed behind him as he closed the door. "That rhymes. Bye, Sky."

Man and dog jogged down the steps and back up to Zoe's place. She'd already put on her coat and held her scarf and hat when she opened the door for them. "Where were you? I didn't see you by my SUV. Is everything all right?"

"Relax." He inhaled a deep breath and was relieved to see Zoe matching his rhythm to keep her panic at bay. "I replaced the tracker. I hate that he's keeping such close tabs on you, but it's better that he's doing it remotely instead of meeting you face-to-face."

She retreated a step when she saw the bag in his hand. "What's that? Did he leave it on my car?"

"No, babe. This is from your friend Gus across the way." He released Sky to find his bowl of water for a drink and unzipped his coat, catching the photographs that fell out. "I've got a few more items for you to process at the lab."

Zoe followed him to the evidence box sitting on her kitchen island and opened it. She pulled out an envelope and held it open for him to drop the photos into. "Do I want to know what's going on?"

"Knowledge is power, Zo. The more we understand, the harder it will be for this guy to stay anonymous." He set the plastic bag on the counter and finally pulled off his gloves. "I paid a visit to your neighbor, Gus. He fancies himself some kind of photographer."

She hugged the manila envelope to her chest. "Are all these pictures of me?"

"Yeah. Nothing inappropriate, but the volume of photos is disturbing." He looked down over his shoulder at her. "He seems like an innocent, like he doesn't understand how his obsession with you could be construed as a threat. He was less intimidated by me and more interested in petting Sky."

Zoe shrugged. "I don't know what his IQ is, but I imagine it's pretty low. His mother has trained him to do certain jobs. He's on Christmas break now, so he's always around, but there's a school and work center he usually attends during the week. He seems like a big kid to me."

"A big kid in a man's body. With a man's urges that he doesn't know how to act on appropriately." Levi wasn't sure he should share this last bit, but if he wanted honesty from her, he needed to be equally forthright. "He said he watched you changing in your bedroom. We can't dismiss this guy from our list of suspects."

He braced himself for a panic attack, but Zoe seemed to

have slipped into criminalist mode. She pulled on sterile gloves, then grabbed a pen to label and date the envelope before she tucked it inside the box. "Yeah, that makes me uncomfortable. But that had to be several weeks ago. Before the messages started. For a couple of months now, I've closed the blinds as soon as I get home and keep the lights low so that *he* can't see me." Her shoulders lifted with a steadying breath, and she looked toward the window over the sink. "I miss seeing everyone's holiday decorations lit up at night and the snow in the park behind us. But it's a sacrifice I make so I don't feel *his* eyes on me all the time and can't get to sleep."

She wasn't getting enough rest? He found himself reaching for her. "Zoe. Can I help…?"

"What goodies do you have in here?" Had she just shifted away from his touch? Or was she really suddenly that interested in opening the plastic bag on the counter?

Right. He was the one who'd insisted on the impersonal, businesslike relationship between them. "A couple more mementoes you might want to catalog as evidence."

She pulled the discarded cup from the plastic bag and grew pale. "I saw Gus take something out of my trash. I didn't realize he was keeping souvenirs. I imagine the only prints on it will be mine and his. Maybe the server's." Still, she packaged and catalogued that, too.

Then she used the pen to turn the squishy package so that she could study the label. When she pushed on the torn edge of the brown paper that had had been taped around the crushed box, a grayish liquid seeped out. "Ugh." Zoe wrinkled up her nose and put the back of her hand to her mouth. "I don't do so well with some smells these days."

Levi took half a step back as well. He didn't need a dog's nose or a criminalist's expertise to know that something had gotten wet and moldy inside that package. "Gus said it had been sitting in the snow outside your door for a couple of days."

"I never saw it."

"Either Gus picked it up as a souvenir or he sent you a gift but retrieved it when you didn't pick it up."

"This isn't Gus's handiwork." She turned her head to the side and took a deep breath before pointing to the smeared markings on the package. Her hand was shaking a little bit, but her voice was steady. "It's from *him*. There's no postmark on it. No return address. But he types labels like this. He misspells my last name with two *n*'s—Zoe *Stockmann*."

"He delivered this to your doorstep?" Levi tugged on the loose wrapping to see what was inside. "He's been that close to you?"

Zoe grabbed his forearm and pulled his hand back. "Wait. How do we know it's not a bomb or something toxic?"

"Sky is specifically trained to detect explosives and certain chemicals." He glanced over at the dog making himself at home on the rug in front of her couch. "He didn't react to anything in Gus's apartment, and he's not reacting to anything now." He ruthlessly squashed the memory of Sky whining and signaling for his attention in those last seconds before Ahmad's bomb had gone off. "I've learned to trust his nose more than my eyes."

"Okay." Trusting Sky's judgment, if not his, Zoe nodded. With the tape rendered useless by the soaked brown paper, she gently peeled open the package. "His other gifts have been tacky, supposedly romantic things. I wonder what…"

Levi saw the contents the same time as Zoe—a set of gray, yellow and green cotton baby onesies, discolored by mold and moisture. But she was already running around the island to the sink where she barely had time to turn the water on before leaning over and retching up the contents of her stomach.

"Oh, my God." She wiped her mouth with the back of her hand but stayed bent over the sink. "Oh, my God."

Levi was beside her in an instant, reaching for her without even thinking. "Easy, babe. Easy." He pulled her long hair off her shoulders and held it back for her in case she got sick again. He filled a glass with water and handed it to her to rinse out her mouth, then rested that hand between her shoulder blades, rubbing soothing circles there. "You're okay. He can't hurt you."

He wasn't sure if it was the mildewy stench or the gift itself that hit him like a punch to the gut. With Zoe's sensitive stomach, she had to be feeling the shock even more profoundly.

"This is the worst yet." Zoe took another sip of water and straightened. "How does he know I'm pregnant? That's what it means, doesn't it? He knows."

Levi released her hair but kept his hand at the small of her back. Screw *impersonal*. He hated seeing the anguish in those pretty blue eyes. "I don't know, babe. I wish I had answers for you. We'll get them, I promise. I won't let him hurt you or the baby."

She glanced back over at the package. "Is there a note? He always sends a note."

He waited for her to nod that she had the glass and her physical reaction under control before he moved away. After pulling one glove back on, he carefully lifted the baby clothes and pulled out the soggy card underneath them. The ink had run, but the typed message was still legible. He read it out loud.

"*Congratulations, Mama.*

Followed you to the doctor's office. An ob-gyn?

Did I guess right?

I don't know if I'm mad that you cheated on me or if I'm happy to have one more name to add to my list.

Baby Stockmann."

Levi swore like the battled-hardened Marine he was.

"No." He turned at Zoe's heartbreaking wail.

"It's not gonna happen," he swore. "I'm not going to let anything happen to you or the baby." She was staring blankly at the middle of his chest. He brushed aside the hair that fell onto her face and tucked it behind her ears before he hunched down so he could look her straight in the eye. "What list is he talking about?"

Her blue eyes blinked and focused on him. "One of the first things he sent me, right after Dad's accident, was a list of people in my life. Family. Coworkers. He'd already scratched out Dad's name. It was titled 'How to Hurt Zoe.' Your sister's name is on the list. My brothers and their wives. My nieces and nephews. They don't even live in Kansas City, but *he* knows about them."

He cupped the sides of her neck and gently cradled her jaw between his palms. "Am I on the list?"

She shook her head.

"Then maybe *he* doesn't know about me yet. That could work to our advantage."

There were no tears, but her breath sounded like a sob. "If *he* doesn't know about you yet, *he* will. *He* always knows."

"Until *he* does, I'm your secret weapon." Levi stroked his thumb across her soft pink lips, remembering the fire of the kiss they'd shared last night, willing her to remember how passionate, how confident she'd been in his arms. "Keep it together, Zo. I need your brain working on this with me." He straightened, forcing her to tilt her head to keep her eyes on his. "Could this be from Gus? You think he was playing me when I talked to him?"

Her fingers crept up to wrap around his wrists, promising she was here in the moment with him. "To be honest, I wouldn't think Gus Packard is bright enough to put together this degree of harassment. I mean, just the commitment of time doesn't feel like something he'd have the patience for. And there's some understanding of technology involved. Finding my new phone number. Sending texts. Typing letters."

"What else has he got to do?" Levi posed. "Watching you has become his hobby. Plus, he has a laptop and a pretty nice camera. I didn't see a printer there, but that doesn't mean it wasn't in another room. He doesn't have to be a brainiac. He just has to have the obsession and opportunity to do it. We know he has both."

She briefly squeezed her hands more tightly around him before stepping away from his touch and hugging her arms around her middle. "Not reassuring."

"Honestly, he's not at the top of my list of suspects. But he could have been feeding me a line so I'd go easier on him. I recruited his help to watch the apartment complex so he checks in with me regularly, and I can keep tabs on him." He hoped his next question wouldn't send her back into panic mode. "I don't suppose you know a man with gray hair who drives a noisy car? Gus says he doesn't live here but he shows up every Wednesday and Friday. Watches until you come home, then leaves."

"You think that's *him*? Here?"

"Gus says he takes pictures of you, then calls someone. Sounds like a private investigator to me. Your perp could have hired him. If we can believe Gus."

"Ethan has gray hair. Prematurely gray. He told me he was completely gray before he turned thirty." She picked up a new evidence bag. "But he's in prison. I know he is. I check his status every week." She slid the package of baby clothes and wrapping into the bag and folded it shut before she took another breath. "You don't think someone's dressing up like him to try to spook me, do you?"

"Have you ever seen this guy?"

She shook her head and paused in the middle of labeling the bag. "Do you think Gus made him up so you'd leave him alone?"

"I'm not counting anybody or anything out until I know more."

"How are you going to learn more?"

"First, you're going to process this evidence and have someone else you trust take a look at it with you. Then you're going to talk to Aiden and get an investigation started. Meanwhile, I'll be driving down to Jefferson City to meet your ex in person. I'll try to find out if he hired someone to harass you or if he called in a favor from a friend to keep tabs on you."

"What if that just antagonizes him?" She finished labeling the bag and reached for a small envelope to drop the card into.

"And what if it's not him? Any information we can get at this point, any suspect we can eliminate helps us. It puts us one step closer to identifying this monster and getting *him* out of your life."

She shivered as she closed the box. "Don't believe anything Ethan says to you." She warned. "He is a master manipulator. He lies as easily as he says his name." She tilted her face up to his once more. "But you're not a guy who trusts what anyone says to you, are you?"

"My skepticism has served me well over the years when I'm working a case." She nodded as if she'd expected such an answer. "I'll follow you to the lab. We'll sit down with Lexi and tell her everything. Then I'll pick up the marriage license on my way back into town, and we can sign it tonight. I'll make an appointment with the judge for tomorrow."

"And you'll still move in some of your things this evening?"

"Are you okay with that?"

"You're not giving me much choice." She reached inside her oversized coat to rub her belly. "But yeah, we're okay with that." She glanced down at Sky, who had recognized the signs of leaving and trotted over to join them. "It'll be nice to have a guard dog on the premises. And a Marine."

"Remember, don't leave the lab by yourself." He hooked

Sky up to his leash and picked up the evidence box. "And if you hear from this douchebag again, let me know. I'll call when I'm back in town."

"Levi?" She stopped him with a hand on his arm. "Could I… Could we…have a hug?" When he hesitated, she quickly retreated to loop her purse over her shoulder and pull out her keys. "That's okay. I shouldn't push. I know you don't trust me anymore. Thank you for…oof."

Levi had dropped the box on the table and pulled her in for a hug. He whispered against her ear, "We're going to get this guy, Zo. Hang in there and be strong. I'll make sure you and the little one are safe."

Her arms crept around his waist and grabbed fistfuls of the back of his coat. Nothing in his life had ever felt as good as holding Zoe. Feeling her strong hands clutching at him and her body softening against him, except for the rounded little pooch where his child rested between them, was like an infusion of life's blood for Levi. For a few precious seconds they clung tightly to each other, and everything felt right. The urge to tug on her hair and tip her head back for a kiss surged through him.

But rational thought crept in around the calming, centering gift of Zoe's touch, and he set her away as abruptly as he'd pulled her into his arms. He couldn't buy into the lie that they were meant to be together anymore, not when she'd so readily pushed him away. He couldn't survive the hope for a happily-ever-after before getting his heart ripped out of his chest again.

"Let's go." He picked up the evidence box and Sky's leash and waited for her to lock up before following her down to her car.

"Be safe today, Levi," she said before rolling up her window and driving away.

"You, too, Zo," he whispered. "Both of you, be safe."

He reached across the cab of the truck to pet Sky and felt his own anxiety level recede a bit. But the thoughts that plagued him were still there.

He'd find Zoe's stalker. He'd give her and the baby his name.

And then, he'd figure out how the hell he was going to make a life with a woman he couldn't trust.

Chapter Nine

Ethan Wynn could have been a professor at a small, ivy-covered college. His thick hair was completely gray, although Levi guessed he was only a few years older than him. He wasn't particularly tall, and his average build leaned more toward bookworm rather than a man who had physically overpowered and strangled three women. And he had a habit of deliberately pushing his black-framed glasses up on his nose with one finger.

It was easy to see how he had flown under the radar without anyone suspecting him of the violence his sister had barely survived and why someone like Zoe would think he was a *safe* man to get involved with.

The amused smile Ethan Wynn greeted Levi with didn't reach his eyes. Levi instantly got the feeling that Wynn believed he was smarter than everybody else in the room. "Who are you? I was hoping for a conjugal visit or my attorney showing up with some good news about my appeal at the very least. Do I know you? Do I want to?"

Levi pulled out the chair on his side of the table and sat. He wondered if he'd get any straight answers out of Wynn. For Zoe and the baby's sake, he had to try. He erased the emotion from his face and tamped down the urge to wrap his hands around the man's throat. "Levi Callahan, Master Sergeant, US Marine Corps."

Wynn's smile broadened. He shifted in his seat, as if he was getting comfortable for the conversation. "Callahan, hmm? Lexi's big brother? I see the family resemblance now. You a self-righteous do-gooder like she is?"

He didn't even bristle at the lame insult. "I'm the one asking the questions today."

Wynn chuckled. "Well, I won't be the one answering them. You're not a cop or a district attorney. You can't compel me to do so."

"No, but you're going to want to." Levi let that teaser hang in the air long enough that Wynn clasped his hands together and leaned forward.

"How so? Is this a military investigation? Let me guess—you found a dead woman who happens to be a Navy lieutenant or a Marine Corps grunt. Well, it wasn't me." He glanced around at the drab beige walls of the prison. "I've got a solid alibi for the past three and a half years."

Levi folded his arms across the plaid flannel shirt he wore. "This isn't a military investigation. But someone is copying you on the outside, using your playbook to terrorize another woman. You strike me as a man who has an ego. I figure you'd either want to take credit for it or find out who's doing your psychological-abuse shtick."

Wynn eyed the defensive stance. Then he nodded. "This is something personal for you." When Levi didn't immediately respond, Wynn sat back and smugly adjusted his glasses again. "You here to warn me away from your sister? It's a little late for that. Lexi and that cop husband of hers and his stupid dog have already taken their shots at me. Any appeals my attorney has filed are legit. All that evidence against me was tainted— by my coworkers who had it in for me."

Silently cheering inside, Levi nodded at the intel Wynn was sharing with him. Revenge could be a motive for Wynn to go after Zoe, Lexi and his former coworkers at the crime lab. Or the desire to scare them out of testifying against him at a possible new trial was an equally compelling motive. "You think you can convince them to reopen the case and clear your name?"

"I wouldn't trust any of them to do that. They resented my superior expertise at the lab. And they all know the only reason your sister got promoted over me was because she's a woman and the department had to meet a quota."

Levi's fingers curled into his palms, and his nostrils flared with the urge the ram his fist into the middle of this misogynistic psychopath's mouth. "So, you're punishing them for doing their job and putting you away where you belong?"

Wynn arched his gray eyebrows above his glasses. "Punishing? Hmm. Is that what your copycat is doing? I like the sound of that." He shrugged. "But I'm afraid I have no idea what you're talking about. My cousin Arlo, who's as close to me as a brother, and my attorney are handling all that for me. I'm just here being a model prisoner."

This guy was probably manipulating someone to do his dirty work for him. "Is one of them your connection to the outside, Wynn? How are you getting messages out?"

"Outside of prison? I don't have that many friends on the outside. My cousin, my attorney. A couple of fangirls who write me letters. I'm allowed to respond. Some of them are quite…passionate…about their feelings for me."

"Did your cousin or attorney hire a private investigator to spy on your former coworkers?"

"I don't know."

"Did one of your *passionate* pen pals hire someone?"

"I have no control over what's going on in the outside world."

"I can request the records of everyone who has come to see you."

"By all means. Ask about the letters, too. The guards open

everything before it comes to me." Wynn leaned forward, steepling his hands in thoughtful pose. "Let's see, did your sister accuse me of some kind of harassment? I'm sure I'm not the only enemy she's made over the years." Levi remained silent, but the other man didn't miss the deep breath he took to calm his temper. Ethan Wynn's subtle smile warned Levi that he'd given away his emotional connection to this interview. The other man snapped his fingers and sat back. "No. You're here because of little Zoe, aren't you? Or her father. How is big ol' Brian Stockman, by the way? I hear he's having a little trouble getting around these days."

"You hear?" Levi repeated. "I thought you didn't have any connections to the outside world."

"I read newspapers. Seems Brian had himself a bad accident."

"What do you know about Brian Stockman's so-called accident?"

Wynn ignored the question, and Levi silently cursed, feeling the balance of power in the room subtly changing. "How is our Zoe? She probably can't function if Daddy's hurt. Is she trying to solve the case?" he mocked. "She was a rookie in every sense of the word. I tried to take her under my wing and mentor her. But—"

"You abused her trust."

"—she had a hard time standing up for herself. Couldn't work independently." Hell, alone and independent was the way she'd been living her entire life the past few months. "Has she washed out of forensic work yet?"

"She's a valued member of the crime lab. Unlike you."

The other man chuckled. "Oh, this is priceless. This isn't about work or finding out how her daddy got hurt. Are you the new man in Zoe's life? Now this visit makes sense. She's unhappy, and you're trying to make it all better for her. How's that going for you? Such a paranoid nervous Nellie. Does she shiver and shake when you try to touch her? I remember her getting all shy and stuttering just when things were starting to heat up. Or she'd lie there like a statue. Hard to make love to a zombie—"

"Shut up!" Levi sprang to his feet, pounding his fist on the table. He could barely hear Wynn's laughter through the angry haze that stuffed his ears like cotton. The guard quickly moved forward. When the man put his hand on Levi's arm, he shrugged it off, then put his hands up in surrender. "I'm good."

"You sure?" the guard asked. "This guy pushes buttons."

Levi nodded. "I'm done." He spared Wynn one last accusing look before heading for the door.

As the door closed, Wynn called after him. "It gives me great pleasure to know that my former colleagues aren't enjoying any happily-ever-afters without me."

Levi grabbed his stuff, signed out and stormed away from the prison. Wynn was behind this somehow. Terrorizing Zoe. Hurting the people she loved. Threatening their unborn baby.

He wasn't sure how yet. But Wynn had to have somebody on the outside acting on his behalf. When Levi got back to KC, he'd talk to his sister and Aiden and request the prison's visitors log, plus see if they could track Wynn's incoming and outgoing mail. The man was too calm about everything—too amused by Levi's protective reaction to the insults he'd shot at Zoe.

Even with the damp, chilly air, Levi's blood was boiling. He felt useless. A step behind. Out of the loop. How the hell was he supposed to protect Zoe and the baby when he couldn't manage his own damn temper? Ethan Wynn had played him like he was a wet-behind-the-ears corporal on his first day of MP duty.

When he opened the door to his truck, he met Sky's dark eyes and heard the whine that said he knew Levi wasn't fit to report for duty and manage this assignment. "I screwed up, boy. I let the enemy get in my head. People are going to get hurt because I can't get the job done anymore."

Sky pushed his black nose into Levi's gloved hands, then lifted his head to lick him across the chin.

"I know. Get over it," he translated, reading into the dog's behavior. "People are counting on me." Sky licked him again. "You're right, pal. Counting on *us*. Come on. Let's do a lap."

He hooked up Sky and jogged with the dog around the parking lot, cooling off his body if not the fever of guilt and frustration still roiling in his brain. When they were back in the truck, Levi gripped the steering wheel tightly. He needed to get the name of that veterans' counseling group his sister had mentioned. He was just too damn volatile lately. And that wasn't doing him any favors. Losing his temper at the wrong moment wouldn't help Zoe and the baby, either. Sky sat in the passenger seat, watching him, perhaps willing him to think of other ways to calm himself down so that he could relax, too. "Sorry, pal. I'll do better."

The German shepherd tilted his head, as if he wanted Levi to prove it.

Levi reached over to scrub the dog's muzzle and ears, remembering a time when he'd been happier, when he'd trusted himself and his ability to do the right thing. He let go of the resentment that had been eating away at him for weeks, and he knew the answer.

Zoe.

He needed her. He needed the woman he'd loved last summer.

He peeled off his gloves and pulled out his phone to send a text.

Can you talk?

He kept his hand on top of Sky's warm head, watching his screen and waiting for her reply. Instead of his screen lighting up with a text, his phone rang. Sky woofed, seemingly approving of the sound before he curled into a ball and lay down with his head resting on the center console.

Levi didn't even get a greeting out before he heard Zoe's shy voice. "Is everything okay? Ethan got under your skin, didn't he? What happened?"

He inhaled a deep breath and slowly released it, calming at hearing her on the other end of the line.

"Levi? Please talk to me."

"I just wanted to know how you were doing." His own voice sounded deep and a little rusty to his ears. "Make sure nothing else has happened."

"I... I'm okay."

"Tell me about your day." It was a question he'd often asked back when they'd been regularly communicating with each other during his last deployment. He liked hearing her voice and gauging her mood to see if she was having a good day or if her anxiety had gotten the better of her.

"I'm running some tests in the lab. Looking for DNA matches on a blob of toothpaste. Hectic morning, but it's settled into a pretty routine afternoon." Even though she couldn't see him, he nodded, liking that she was able to have some *routine* time for a change. "After our meeting with Lexi and Aiden this morning, she told everyone on my team about the baby, and they've been congratulating me. Chelsea is already planning a baby shower." Levi recognized the name of the crime lab's resident hacker and computer guru. "They're going to hold it right here in the staff lounge. She's been online looking up what the safest cribs, car seats and high chairs are. She printed off a report for me. We can decide which ones to get. Together. If you want."

He nodded again. "Yeah, I want to do that."

She hesitated for a second. But now that he was hearing her voice, the rage and frustration inside him had abated to a level he could manage. "Lexi told them about my stalker, too. The guys are all being super protective of me. I'm still scared that the more people who know, the more people are in danger...because of me."

"Just the opposite, Zo." He found the strength to reassure her. "It means more eyes to watch your back. More phone numbers to call if you need help."

Her heavy sigh told him she wasn't totally convinced that sharing the threats she'd been receiving was a good idea. He listened for any hint that her anxiety was taking over, but his Zoe was a brave woman. She'd told him her struggles were easier to cope with when she could focus on something out-side of herself. It felt good to realize she was focused on him. "It sounds like Ethan said something that upset you."

Levi scoffed at his own hubris to think he'd been ready to go toe-to-toe with someone as devious as Ethan Wynn. "You were right. He does know how to push buttons."

Her gentle, wry laugh felt like a caress. "I warned you. What can I do to help?"

"You're doing it. Just talking to me. Listening. Maybe be-cause you're so naturally quiet and level-headed, it calms me. I've missed this."

"I have, too. I... I should have handled things differently between us. My intention was never to hurt you."

"Don't. No more apologies. You were protecting our child. I can never fault you for that."

"But can you forgive me?" she asked.

"I'm working on it," he answered, knowing he owed her some apologies, too. "Be patient with me."

She laughed again. "That's the pot calling the kettle black. I'm working on, too." He heard her tone hush and imagined her wrapping her arms around her waist for comfort. "I'm sorry Ethan upset you."

"Don't be. After spending a few minutes with that creep, I

get why you made the choices you did. I'm the one who needs to change the way I react to things. I'm sorry I've been a jerk to you. Making declarations and accusations? Throwing an engagement ring at you?"

"You haven't—"

"Yeah, babe, I have." The endearment rolling off his tongue sounded familiar, natural, right. "I plan to stop by that veterans' support group at St. Luke's Hospital after I finish my errands. Maybe I do have some PTSD. I seem to have anger-management issues I never did before."

"Talking with my therapist has helped me with my anxiety issues. At least, I... I have tools to help me cope when I get overwhelmed now."

He was glad to hear that. "That's a good recommendation. Thanks."

"Are you on the road yet? Are you in the right headspace to drive safely?"

"As soon as I pull out of here, I'm leaving Jefferson City. I'll still have time to stop at the courthouse to pick up the license."

Yeah. Calling Zoe had been the right thing to do. He glanced over at Sky and imagined his know-it-all dog rolling his eyes and saying, *Told you so.* Levi reached over and petted him. Guard dog, explosives detector and now K-9 therapist. He grinned at his furry partner and mouthed the words *Thank you.*

Then he turned his attention back to the phone. "Make sure someone walks you to your car. Drive straight to your apartment. Call me when you're safely inside."

"I will."

After sharing some serious conversation and absorbing her gentleness and support, he was more than ready to hit the road.

"Are you still moving some stuff in tonight?" she asked.

"After the meeting, I'll swing by Lexi and Aiden's and pack my gear and Sky's. We'll leave the furniture for the weekend."

"But where will you sleep?"

"On your couch. Trust me, I've slept in worse places."

"But—"

"It'll be fine," he said.

"I'll fix us some dinner. Pasta okay?"

"With your homemade red sauce?"

"Yeah."

"Sounds good," he said.

"I'll see you at home," she said.

Home. Sounded nice. He wished it was a permanent thing. But for now, he'd take what he could get.

"Yeah. See you there."

Chapter Ten

Zoe hooked the two grocery bags over her forearm, looped her purse around her neck and shoulder, stuffed her gloves in her coat pocket, climbed out of her SUV and butted the door shut with her hip while she started her text to Levi.

I'm sorry I'm late getting home. (In case you were worried why I hadn't checked in yet.) Don't be mad. I stopped at the grocery store after work. I haven't felt like cooking in a while, and I realized my cupboards—

"Hey, neighbor!"

Zoe startled at the cheery voice from the other side of her SUV and threw herself against her side of the car, knocking her arm against the side-view mirror. In her efforts to catch her phone and keep it from landing in the snow drift next to the curb, her purse shifted, knocking one of the plastic bags off her arm. Canned goods hit the pavement and rolled out of the bag, along with some items she'd picked up in the health-and-beauty-aids department and a quart of caramel-swirl ice cream.

Zoe took a quick assessment of herself and her surroundings, breathed cold air in through her nose and out through her mouth to try to calm her racing heart. But as soon as she acknowledged the fear that robbed her of breath and could push it aside to allow in a rational thought, she realized the friendly greeting came from a familiar woman's voice—not that creepy mechanical tone that usually terrorized her.

"Zoe? Boy, are you jumpy. Is everything okay?"

When the older blonde woman came around the front of the vehicle, she knew she'd overreacted. "Poppy. Sorry. I was in the middle of texting. You startled me."

"Oh, sweetie, I'm so sorry. I guess you didn't hear me pull in beside you." Poppy Hunter wore what looked like a scarlet skiing ensemble with fitted quilted pants, a matching short jacket, a white knit scarf and mittens and oversized earmuffs that reminded her of a famous science-fiction princess.

Zoe couldn't help but feel a little jealous that her neighbor was dressed for winter fun while she'd spent most of her favorite time of the year hiding behind locked doors. "That's okay. I was paying attention to my phone and not what was going on around me. I know better."

Poppy squatted down beside her and started gathering items. "Here, let me help."

"Thanks." Zoe awkwardly dropped down to her knees to reach the tub of ice cream that had rolled beneath her SUV.

She had just shaken open the sack and put the ice cream inside when Poppy grabbed Zoe's left wrist and pulled it up in front of her face, letting out a high-pitched squeal of excitement. "Is this what I think it is? Diamond ring. Third finger. Left hand. Are you getting married?"

Although she cringed at being grabbed like that, Zoe gently extricated herself from her friend's curious grasp. She couldn't very well keep it a secret when Poppy had already seen the evidence for herself. "Levi…" He hadn't exactly proposed, and remembering that *for the baby* stipulation put a little chink in the good mood she'd been in since his phone call from Jefferson City. "He gave it to me last night."

Poppy didn't seem to think there was anything wrong with

Zoe's explanation. She scooped up a couple more items and dropped them into the sack. But she kept hold of one plastic bottle and read the contents. "Prenatal vitamins?" She hugged the bottle to her chest and squealed again. "Are you...? Girl... you sure know how to keep a secret. No wonder he proposed." She rose up on her knees and leaned over to give Zoe a fierce hug. "Congratulations! When are you due? Everything going okay?"

Zoe plucked the vitamins from her neighbor's hand and tried to quiet her down. "Poppy, please. It's not common knowledge yet."

Poppy pantomimed zipping her red lips shut and throwing away the key. Thankfully, she dropped her voice to a normal volume and linked her elbow with Zoe's to help her stand. "I just thought you were gaining some winter weight. We all do." She released Zoe and fell into step beside her as they headed to their building. "But now that I've met your fella, it makes sense. You finally got your baby daddy to do the right thing."

Zoe didn't like the implication that Levi had shirked his responsibilities. "Levi was a deployed Marine. Stationed overseas. He couldn't be here. But the moment he got home, he came to see me. He's a good, honorable man."

"Whoa, whoa. I didn't mean anything by it. I'm just speaking from my own experience. The good ones don't stay around if the going gets tough."

Zoe paused on the bottom step, looking up at her taller friend. "I'm sorry to hear that. But I'm a little confused. I know you love your jewelry. I thought one of those rings you wear was an engagement ring."

Poppy blushed and removed her glove, showing all the rings on her left hand, including the rather showy diamond solitaire surrounded by a circle of smaller stones on her third finger. She turned her hand until it caught the weak winter light and sparkled. "Isn't it beautiful? It's a promise ring, I suppose, until he's ready to get married."

Wow. That was some promise. If this was just the precursor, she couldn't imagine how gaudy Poppy's actual engagement ring might be. But a promise and not an engagement ring? Was the man buying trinkets for her friend and stringing her along?

The older woman leaned closer and whispered. "It's manmade. We didn't want to spend a fortune on a diamond. And I could get something bigger with a lab-grown stone. You know how I love my bling."

We bought the ring? Zoe supposed it wasn't any of her business how Poppy split expenses with her boyfriend. Or even if she chose to see someone who wouldn't fully commit to her. Maybe they just couldn't afford the kind of wedding they wanted yet. "It's still a beautiful ring. Personally, I like that it's different. It's an original."

Poppy held her hand up and studied it for a moment before pulling her gloves back on. "Like me, huh?" Zoe worried that she just offended her friend, but Poppy laughed at her own joke. "He's awfully clever, don't you think? Not another one like him."

"I hope I get to meet him soon."

"I do, too." Poppy sighed and started up the stairs. "His work takes him out of town quite a lot, but he always stays in touch—a phone call, a text, a letter. Absence makes the heart grow fonder, I suppose. When we do get together, we practically combust."

"That's great. I'm happy for you, Poppy." Zoe dredged up a smile for her neighbor as they reached her door on the first landing. "I'd better get inside and get dinner started."

"Ah, domestic bliss. You're a lucky woman, Zoe. And congratulations again on the baby. Don't be surprised if a little gift shows up on your doorstep."

Zoe shivered at the thought, remembering the baby clothes from this morning. She was really starting to hate receiving gifts. "You don't have to do that."

"Are you kidding? Who else can I go baby shopping for? You think I'm going to get pregnant at my age?"

She'd always assumed that Poppy was in her forties. Could the heavy makeup and stylish clothes be hiding a more significant age gap? "You're not that old."

Poppy smiled. "Bless you for lying like that."

"You could always adopt," Zoe suggested.

Her neighbor shrugged. "I've thought about it. But I intend to be married first. In the meantime, let me spoil you a little bit."

It might be nice to have other people excited about the baby. Maybe then Zoe could channel their excitement and enjoy her pregnancy more—and not be so worried about keeping the baby safe. "If you insist." If she had a free hand, she'd be cradling her belly right now because she *did* have to worry about keeping her baby safe.

Zoe stopped her friend before she headed up to the second floor. "Hey, Poppy. Have you seen a gray-haired man watching our building?"

"A gray-haired man?" With mock eagerness, Poppy moved to the railing at the edge of the landing and swept her gaze across the parking lot. "Is he new here? Is he married?"

Um, hadn't she just mentioned receiving a ring from a boyfriend? Zoe frowned at the woman's enthusiasm. "I have no idea. But he doesn't live here. Gus, across the way, said he sees him parked in our lot every Wednesday and Friday. Taking pictures?"

"I'll keep a look out for him tomorrow, then." Poppy's smile disappeared. She turned her gaze to Zoe, then circled around, scanning the entire complex. "Wait. What's he taking pictures of? Us? Oh, my God, is he a Peeping Tom? Do you think he's casing our apartment complex?"

Zoe wasn't sure she was up to explaining about having a stalker. She'd already strayed too far out of her comfort zone by confirming Poppy's guesses about her being pregnant and engaged. "I have no idea. I was just wondering if we should be concerned, if there was any merit to Gus's claim."

"Oh, well, you can't put much stock in anything Gus Packard says." But Poppy wasn't smiling any longer. "Still, if I see that gray-haired man, I'll call the police and report him."

"I'll do the same. Thanks."

Poppy made an exaggerated shiver. "Be sure you lock your door up tight. I don't know how many other single women live in our complex. But hearing that someone might be spying on us is a little unsettling."

After saying good night and locking the door behind her, Zoe kicked off her boots and hung up her coat. She carried her groceries into the kitchen and quickly stuck the ice cream in the freezer. The rest could wait until she made the rounds through her apartment. She was glad that she'd finally gotten rid of that box of letters and gifts. Her memories and imagination were vivid enough for her to believe she was being watched around the clock without the tangible reminders staring her in the face.

She flipped on the lamp beside the couch and went to the windows to draw the blinds. She couldn't help but picture Gus at his window, looking at her through his binoculars. Trying not to feel that sense of violation, she pressed her back against the wall beside the window and quickly drew the curtains. Her nostrils flared as she inhaled a jagged breath. Although Gus didn't seem to understand how uncomfortable she was being the object of his interest—even after what she was sure had been an intimidating visit from Levi and Sky—he wasn't really a threat, was he? Was his claim about the gray-haired man spying on her just a story he'd made up in his head?

Moving through the apartment to close the blinds and curtains in the other rooms, she thought about how much her life had changed in the past few months. Even in the past few days. She'd been so happy this summer, certain she'd found the love of her life. And then *he* had made his presence known.

She'd discovered she was pregnant. She'd broken Levi's heart.

She'd sacrificed her own happiness in the name of staying safe.

But now Levi was back in her life. She was marrying him. He was happy about the baby if not ready to completely trust her yet.

Yet *she* was the one he'd called this afternoon when he'd been so upset by his meeting with Ethan Wynn. He needed her. For a woman who felt like she'd been a burden to everyone else her entire adult life, being needed was heady stuff. Treating her as if she was strong made her feel stronger.

They were partners. A team. She almost felt like they were a couple again. Although she knew they might never get back to that madly in love couple they'd been last summer, she was happy to have Levi in her life again.

Feeling more hopeful than she had for the past few months, Zoe pulled her pink fuzzy slipper socks from under her pillow and tugged them on over the socks she wore to keep her toes warm. Then she'd go out to the kitchen to unload the groceries and start dinner.

But she'd barely pulled her pants back up after a bathroom break when her phone rang in her pocket. Oh, shoot. She'd forgotten to finish her text to Levi. He was probably wondering why she was so late getting home. She quickly pulled out her phone and saw the number.

Unknown.

So much for hope.

Had *he* gotten another disposable phone with a new number?

Her lips and fingers trembled as a chill shivered through her body. The panic she'd foolishly pushed aside for a short time squeezed her lungs in a tight grip. This was the reprimanding call she'd risked by disobeying *his* order to come straight home from work. She had the presence of mind to peek through the blinds to make sure Gus had closed up his spy shop across the way. Although his window was dark, she felt no relief. Now that she couldn't see him, she had no way of knowing where he was or what he was up to.

Bracing herself for that raw, mechanical voice, she swept her finger across the screen and whispered. "Hello?"

"What the hell do you think you're doing, sending your boyfriend to Jefferson City to harass my cousin?"

She should have felt better that it was a real man's voice on the line. Instead, it was an angry voice, attacking her psyche from a different direction.

Zoe sank onto the edge of the bed as the harangue continued. "Arlo."

She pulled the phone from her ear and punched the button to end the call. Then she opened the drawer of her bedside table and pulled out the handheld recorder her therapist had encouraged her to use when she woke up in a panic and couldn't calm herself down, to get out of her head and count out loud or talk about whatever had set her off. She clicked *Record* and held it up near her phone because she knew…

Her phone vibrated in her hand and started ringing again. She wasn't surprised that Arlo had called her right back after hanging up on him. Apparently, all the Wynn men knew how to break a person down with their endless harassment.

This time she was prepared when she answered. "Hello, Arlo."

"How dare you!" Arlo yelled, his contemptuous tone sounding so much like Ethan's. "You're as bad as your boyfriend, being rude. You can't harass Ethan, and you shouldn't ignore me."

"He didn't." She had no idea what had been said between Ethan and Levi, but she was certain Ethan would have been the aggressor, seeking out Levi's weak spots and poking at them with cruel, taunting words. "I answered your call, didn't I?"

"No woman has the right to disrespect me like that."

She bowed her head, and the words *I'm sorry* danced on the tip of her tongue.

But Arlo Wynn never gave her a chance to say them. "Ethan has been a model prisoner. You and your boyfriend are drawing negative attention to him, and that won't help his appeal. You're supposed to stand by your man, to love him."

Yeah, um, her man. That wouldn't be Ethan. Not anymore. Maybe he never had been hers. She'd just been a possession to him, another tool in his arsenal of manipulation games. He'd been grooming her to be blindly loyal. But she wasn't. She was just so tired of fighting this harassment. She tried to listen to the logical side of her brain. "His appeal is going to fail. The c-case against him was r-rock solid. It wasn't j-just me." Oh damn, she was starting to hyperventilate. She squeezed her eyes shut and tried to count. Inhale, hold it. One, two, three… The memory of Ethan's bruising grip on her arms interrupted her efforts. Instead of numbers, she heard *his* words in her head, belittling her, calling her useless and spineless and messed up in the head. "Ethan hurt me. He scared me."

"Because you screwed up." Arlo took a breath and went on. "But you can make things right. One word from you and he won't be rotting away in prison anymore."

She shook aside the image of her tormentor and tried to picture Levi's steady green eyes and deep, gentle voice counting with her, calming her. She imagined his strong arms wrapping around her. "I took an oath to the crime lab and KCPD. I couldn't lie and give him an alibi."

"The hell you couldn't. If I ever get my hands on you, you'll regret it." The comforting image faded away. Not even Ethan's face or Arlo's threats filled her head. There was only blackness and uncertainty and fear. "Think of everything he taught you. You owe him, you stupid little..."

Her anxiety was a relentless beast once it took hold. Zoe felt herself shutting down. She didn't hear the rest of the conversation details, only the voice of a man yelling at her and criticizing her, until eventually, she heard nothing at all.

LEVI'S CONNECTIONS TO KCPD and the crime lab wouldn't help him if he got pulled over speeding back to Zoe's apartment complex from the mall where he'd stopped to purchase a surprise gift for her. He knew he was going way too fast.

Something was wrong. He'd taken too long to get back to her, spent too long at the St. Luke's Hospital therapy session, hanging around afterward and getting to know some of the other veterans—and now she might've been paying the price for his negligence. There'd been no text from her, letting him know she'd gotten home okay. And she hadn't answered any of the three times he'd attempted to call her.

As much as he loathed the idea that *he* had somehow gotten his hands on her, Levi couldn't help that suspicious nagging in the pit of his stomach that she was ghosting him again, that promising to marry him and pulling him out of his angry funk when he'd called from Jeff City earlier hadn't meant a thing to her. That conversation had meant the world to him. He thought they'd moved past some of the hurts between them, that they'd grown closer. Even though her reasons might've been noble, to protect him and the baby, he thought he'd broken through her defenses and convinced her that shutting him out was not the way to keep any of them safe—and that it only hurt their relationship when she kept secrets from him. Now he was getting nothing but silence again.

Levi's truck kicked up slush and snow from beneath his tires as he whipped around the corner into the parking lot of Zoe's apartment complex.

He spotted her pink SUV and literally growled as he parked as close to it as possible. Leaving his duffel bag in the back seat to retrieve later, he grabbed his packages and hauled Sky out of the truck, scoping out the buildings as they jogged toward her vehicle. He caught a flicker of movement at Gus Packard's window, but since he spotted no camera or binoculars, he'd cut the young man a break and focused on getting to Zoe.

He pulled off a glove and stopped at her SUV, resting his hand on the hood. Ice cold. So, she'd been home for a while. Clicking his tongue, he urged Sky into a jog beside him and took the stairs to the second floor two at a time.

He jammed his key into the lock and opened the door. Sky danced with anticipation beside him as he closed and locked the door behind him. Either the dog sensed something was off or he was picking up the tension radiating down the lead from Levi.

"Zoe? Sorry I'm late. Things ran longer than I thought they would." Levi set his packages on the table and shrugged off his coat. He was going with Sky's instincts warning him that something wasn't right. There was a lamp on beside the sofa, but no other lights had been turned on. He looked into the kitchen and saw grocery bags that were still full sitting on the counter. One sat in a puddle of melting slush. "Babe, if you're here, I need you to answer me. Zoe?"

His heart thumped loudly in his chest. He could only think of a couple of reasons why she wouldn't answer. And neither of them was good.

Not wasting time fumbling through the shadowy apartment himself, he let the dog off his leash. "Sky, seek."

Slipping into military cop mode, he pulled a chef's knife from the magnetic strip above the stove and gripped its solid handle. Slowing his breathing and calming his heart rate, he listened to Sky's claws clicking over the wood floors, falling silent as he crossed an area rug, then clicking again. Levi inched toward the hallway where Sky's nose was leading him. *Please, God, just don't let her be dead. I can work with anything else. I can make it right—*

His prayer was ended by a loud bark.

Levi was on the move before the excited whining began. The dog had found his target. "Zoe!" Levi entered Zoe's bedroom with the knife at the ready but quickly stood down when he saw the dark bundle curled up in a ball on the rug beside Zoe's bed.

Levi cursed when he saw her sitting there on the floor with her knees hugged up to her chest. Her face was tucked into the tight grip she held on herself, and he could barely make out the words she whispered over and over: "One, two, three, four, five."

Ah, hell. She was trying to pull herself out of a panic attack. He turned on the bedside lamp and set the knife on the table above her head before kneeling beside her. "Zoe? I'm so sorry. What's happened? What's wrong?"

She didn't answer.

"It's me, Zo. It's Levi. I won't let anybody hurt you."

She just kept counting.

"Sky, sit. Down." He unhooked Sky's leash and removed the dog's harness, telling him he was off duty for now. "Good boy. You're my good boy." Still sensing the need to work, intuitively knowing what was needed of him, the German shepherd crept forward on his belly, lying on the rug beside Zoe's hip and leaning into her. "Smartest dog I know. Good job, Sky." He turned his attention back to Zoe's pale expression.

"Do you feel that, Zoe? Sky's here, too. He's worried about you. Can you talk to us? Please?"

He saw her cell phone on the rug between her feet and picked it up. Whoever she'd been talking with had long since disconnected. Hoping she still used the same code on this phone that she'd used last summer, he unlocked it and scrolled through to discover an unknown number had called her twice. He also found the text she'd started to him over an hour ago that had never been sent. She hadn't blown off his concern. He inhaled a deep breath and scolded himself for ever thinking she'd been inconsiderate of his needs or careless with her own safety. Someone or something had interrupted her.

After turning off her phone and tucking it into the back pocket of his jeans, he looked back to see she had uncrossed one of her arms and was squeezing one of those old-fashioned handheld tape recorders in her grip. She let him pry it free before hugging her arm back around her knees.

"What's this?" Levi quickly examined the device. The Record button was still pressed down, although it had clearly reached the end of its tape. He pushed the Rewind button, then hit Play to listen to whatever it was she wanted him to hear. He cursed at the angry male voice berating her, then accusing her of hanging up on him when she stopped responding to his accusations. When he saw her shrinking away , Levi shut off the infernal device and set it on the table above her head.

"I'm sorry, babe. That's good evidence to prove harassment, but you don't need to listen to that again." He didn't want to chase evidence right now, either. He wanted to focus on the situation right in front of him. Ethan Wynn had done this to her. Ethan and whatever minion he'd hired or coerced to do his dirty work on the outside had preyed on this vulnerable woman for the last time. "Zoe? Can you hear me? Do you know who I am?"

She didn't speak, but the long fall of coffee-colored hair stirred across her shoulder as she nodded.

"I'm going to check you out, make sure you're okay. I'm going to touch your neck, okay?" Even though her eyes remained unfocused, her fingers reached over to rest on top of Sky's head. Her skin was cool and clammy, but the pulse in her neck was beating steadily, if a little faster than he'd like. She was curled up so tightly, it was hard to gauge her breathing. "That's right, babe. Sky and I are here with you. You're safe."

Her gaze slid toward him, perhaps only seeing his chest or shoulder. "Sorry," she whispered. "Couldn't... c-couldn't stop..."

"No." The word came out a little more sharply than he'd intended, so he slipped his fingers around to the nape of her neck. "You're not apologizing for anything. None of this is on you." When he felt her lean back into his touch, he exhaled a sigh of relief and bent forward to press his lips against her temple. "I want to hold you now. May I?"

Her nod was stronger this time.

"Come here." Levi slipped his arms around her back and beneath her knees and lifted her into his chest as he stood. Nudging the dog aside, he turned and sat on the edge of the bed, holding her in his lap. "Is this okay?"

She gave him another small nod. Her trust in him was as humbling as it was reassuring. She needed a little time to recover, but she was going to be okay.

Keeping her snug against him, he released her legs and lay back across the bed with her on top of him. "You hold on to me, too. Feel me breathing. Try to breathe with me. In. Out. Slowly."

She rose and fell with every breath until something shuddered through her. Finally, her inhales and exhales synced up with his own.

"That's it. You've got it. You're so brave. So beautiful." He felt her fingers slide across his chest and subtly curl into the front of his flannel shirt and the insulated Henley he wore underneath. "So damn brave."

The counting had stopped, but he felt her pressing her cheek against his shoulder. "Ethan's cousin called…threatened me…"

"Shh. We'll talk later." He tunneled his fingers into her silky dark hair and gently massaged her scalp, feeling his own emotions calming as she relaxed against him. "Right now we're just going to rest. Close your eyes. I've got you."

Her fingers tightened, pinching a little skin on his chest, making him feel needed. Wanted. Reminding him he was lucky to be alive. "I'm so cold."

"Not for long." Levi shifted them on the bed, finding a pillow for his head and freeing the top quilt to wrap it around Zoe before pulling her back to his side. "Sky. Up."

With an easy leap, Sky joined him on top of the quilt and stretched out on the bed behind her. "Warm enough?"

The whisper of her sigh felt like a caress against his neck. "Thank you, Levi. I needed this. Thank you for forgiving me."

"Nothing to forgive, babe. I'm the one who's been an impossible ass—"

Her fingertips scraped over the stubble of his beard and pressed against his lips to silence him. "Uh-uh. You said no talking right now. Just rest."

He kissed her fingers, then her forehead before she tucked herself back against him and drifted off to sleep.

Levi was content enough that he dozed a little bit himself. But about an hour later, when Zoe stirred against him, he was instantly awake. He instinctively tightened his arms around her. "What's wrong?"

"Nothing." She pushed against his chest and tried to roll away, but she was pinned beneath the quilt. "Guys, I'm okay now. I need to start dinner."

"No, you don't."

"Well, I do need to pee." That sounded a little more urgent.

"Sky, down." As soon as the dog jumped down, he pulled back the covers and Zoe scuttled off the bed. When she came in after using the bathroom, he stretched out his arm to her. He wasn't ready to let the close moments they'd shared end yet. Besides, he knew they needed to talk about what had happened. "Please?"

With a soft smile, she laid her hand in his and climbed back onto the bed beside him. "You still have your hat on." She slipped her fingers beneath the knit band of his watch cap and pushed it off his head. "You were that worried about me, hmm?" Her smile broadened as she combed her fingers through the short spikes of his hair. "And now I've messed up your hair." He felt every touch like a caress and treasured her bemused smile. "Are you going to grow it out now that you've left the Marines?"

"I hadn't thought about it."

"What have you thought about?" She pulled her hand away. "Besides whether or not you can ever trust me again."

Levi caught her hand before she completely retreated from him and splayed it over his heart beneath the warmth of his own hand. "I'm trying to move past that," he admitted. "Because I'm pretty damn sure I need you, and I don't want to lose you. And I don't want things to be awkward between us when the baby comes. You're trying hard to get us back to where we used to be. I intend to do the same for you." He squeezed her hand beneath his. "I gave up on us, Zo, and I'm ashamed of that. I won't let it happen again."

"Okay." Her clear blue eyes meeting his did more to reassure him she was past the panic attack and with him one hundred percent. "I won't shut you out again, either. If I do, it's because something's preventing me from talking to you, not because I'm choosing to do so."

"Deal."

She smiled again before tucking her head beneath his chin. He rubbed his fingers up and down her arm, and she shifted onto her side to curl her knee up over his thigh. The position was intimate and trusting and reminded him of the intense week they'd spent together last summer. Of course, that had involved a lot warmer temperatures and a lot fewer clothes. It also reminded him that they were two people who'd once been in love, and he was determined to get them back to that happy, hopeful, supportive place.

For a few minutes they simply held each other. Once he was certain they were both ready to talk about the threat that had sent her into a tailspin, he spoke again. "Think you can tell me what happened now?"

She plucked at a nonexistent fuzz on his shirt, then smoothed it back into place, needing time to gather her thoughts. "Arlo Wynn called. He knows you went to see Ethan. He was pissed, said it's my fault his cousin is in prison. Something to do with his appeal. Like usual, he wanted me to make things right."

"As in, give Ethan an alibi for his attack on Lexi? Or murdering one of those other women?" She nodded. "You think that Arlo is behind these sick threats?"

"I don't know." She didn't sound convinced. "Unless he was trying to throw me off. He yelled at me in his real voice— not that distorted mechanical monster I hear when *he* calls. But Arlo does have gray hair, like Ethan. Maybe he's the guy Gus saw taking pictures of me. Maybe he's spying for Ethan."

"I'll ask Aiden to check him out." Levi shook his head, feeling like he was missing something important that the MP who hadn't yet been betrayed and blown up by a friend would have picked up on. "I have a feeling that whoever is behind this terror campaign is someone you know. Someone who's part of your life, even if it's peripheral. I wish I knew his end game. My gut tells me it's more than getting you to change your testimony against Ethan so he can win his appeal."

"I won't."

"I know." He brushed his fingers through her hair again, loving the feel of the heavy strands against his skin. "You need to keep track of the people around you, the people you talk to every day. If anything seems off to you, anyone makes you uncomfortable, I want to know about it. If I'm not with you, call me. Get yourself away from that person and find your way to me. And know that I will be coming for you as fast as I can. I swear to God, I will keep you safe."

"And the baby?"

"Of course the baby." Hell. This wasn't just about the life they'd created. This was about protecting the woman who owned his heart, the woman he needed in his life. "But this is about *you*. I promise I'm getting over feeling so hurt, feeling like you'd ghosted me when I needed you. I understand why now. And I'm smart enough to know that was nothing like the way I'd feel if something happened to you, if I lost you completely. I…"

He loved her. He knew in his heart that was the truth. He loved Zoe Stockman.

But was he ready to say those words to her? Could he trust that she felt the same way?

He must have paused too long because Zoe pushed herself onto her elbows and kissed the underside of his jaw before sitting up. "It's okay, Levi. You don't have to say any magic words. I feel your caring. I'm grateful for it. I need it to keep going right now." She touched her belly. "We both do. And I promise to do my damnedest to be there for you, too, if you ever need me again." He sat up beside her. "I'm just so tired of dealing with all this." Her stomach gurgled, and they both chuckled. She swung her legs off the side of the bed and stood. "I'd better get us all some dinner before it becomes a bedtime snack. I don't have time to thaw out my pasta sauce like I planned. Soup and sandwiches okay?"

"I'll do it." He was already up and moving around the end of the bed.

Zoe stopped him with a hand in the middle of his chest. "No. I need to be busy right now. Until I have some new evidence to process, I don't want to have so much time to think."

"Then I'll help." He pulled her in for another hug and dropped a kiss to the crown of her hair. "We work together as a team now, remember?"

The tension in him eased when her arms wrapped around his waist and she tucked her head beneath his chin. "My favorite place to be," she whispered.

"Mine, too." Her stomach growled again, and Levi grinned. "Come on. Let's get you and the little one fed."

He kept her hand snugged in his as he led her back to the kitchen, turning on every light they passed along the way. She'd had enough hiding in the darkness just to keep herself and the baby safe. He'd had enough of the darkness living inside his soul, too. Zoe was his light, and he'd do everything in his power to protect that light. He'd meant it when he said they were a team now. And tomorrow they'd be husband and wife.

Chapter Eleven

29 December...

Today was her wedding day.

Zoe was surprised by the anticipation she was feeling this morning. Lexi had agreed to let her take her lunch near the end of the day so she could leave to meet Levi at the courthouse and not have to come back to the lab afterward, keeping all of her leave time intact.

She was at work behind her desk, skimming through reports from the evidence her coworkers had processed for her. The letters she'd received had nary a fingerprint on them, not even her own since she'd been taking precautions to preserve any potential evidence. Same with the presents she'd received, from the gaudy stained-glass ornament to the mildewed package of baby clothes. There were more tests that could be run, but they would have to wait. With a skeleton staff over the holidays and a backlog of other cases the lab was working on, she was grateful for the help she had already received from her coworkers.

She'd even finished her analysis of the random fingerprints she'd found on her father's truck. Turned out there was no match in AFIS, so maybe she should've been glad she wasn't looking for a perpetrator with a criminal record, like Ethan. But that didn't mean there couldn't be a match in another database—the military, teacher screenings, immigrants applying for green-card status and more. She turned the prints over to her friend Chelsea to do a deep research dive into finding a match.

As planned, Zoe was treating this as much like a regular workday as possible while Levi traded some phone calls with Aiden to get information on Arlo Wynn and Gus Packard. Aiden had discovered that Arlo had indeed been a private investigator—in the state of California. But after committing several misdemeanors, his license had been revoked. If he was following Zoe and cataloguing her activities with photographs, then he was doing so illegally and might soon be joining his cousin in prison. Aiden had gotten a plate number for Arlo's car, and he and Levi were taking turns watching the parking lot at her apartment complex to see if he showed up for his regular photography session. Meanwhile, Gus had no record of criminal activity whatsoever. But the information didn't clear either man as a suspect.

Levi had also run some errands to take care of the last-minute preparations for the ceremony. One of those errands included stopping by her office to deliver a sack from a well-known store with a big maternity department. While they didn't carry wedding dresses in-store, he had found a beautiful ivory sweater dress. It might not have screamed *wedding* with a bunch of lace or beading, but it did fit her changing shape. It clung to the top of her figure, hugged her baby bump and draped to a flattering length against her calves. And though Levi had confessed to texting Lexi pictures to help him make the decision, Zoe was more than touched that her big, badass Marine had ventured to the mall to buy a dress for her to wear.

As bad as last night had been with Arlo's call, she was feeling good this morning. She and Levi might've been getting married for the baby's sake, but she was marrying the man she loved. Zoe intended to show Levi she was serious about her commitment to him. Although it wasn't going to be a conventional marriage to begin with, she had to believe that one day it could be.

She closed the reports and stacked them beside the blotter on her desk. Then she got up and opened the closet door in her office where a full-length mirror was attached to the inside of the door. She pulled back the front of her oversized lab coat and studied the dress one more time. Her long johns and wool socks weren't doing her look any favors. But still, this was her wedding dress. Zoe smiled at Levi's thoughtfulness. As crass as his proposal had been, he really was trying to make this a special day for them. She ran her hand over the soft cashmere hugging her baby bump. "We're getting married today, little one. Your daddy and I both love you so much. Our lives are about to change—"

Even her cell phone ringing in the pocket of her coat couldn't douse her optimistic mood. For a few seconds, she thought it must be Levi calling to remind her of something. Or it could be her father, double-checking the time he needed to be at the courthouse or trying one more time to make sure she'd made a rational decision in accepting Levi's sudden proposal.

But when she'd fished the phone out of her pocket and looked at the number, her good mood vanished. She'd programmed the number to show one word on the screen: *Him*.

The familiar fear licked through her veins. But it was chased by a less familiar emotion. Anger.

This was *her* day. And *he* had the gall to ruin that rare feeling of happiness she'd been enjoying? She answered the call just before it went to her voicemail. "What do you want from me?"

The distorted mechanized voice on the other end grated against her nerves and challenged her bravado. "No, no, no, Zoe. *I'm* the one who asks the questions. Why was there a man in your apartment the last two nights? And a dog? They're unclean."

The man or the dog? A few sarcastic brain cells really wanted to verbally spar with this guy. But any sign of defiance could be a risk. And risks weren't her best thing. Better to endure this conversation and get it over with so that she could get on with her day.

Glancing down, she saw the ring on her hand. The diamond and two smaller stones on either side were set down inside a track in the gold ring. It was much less flashy than Poppy Hunter's showy stone but meaningful because Levi had considered how much she worked with her hands and how often she wore sterile gloves. It was personalized and thoughtful and reminded her just how much she loved the big bruiser with the tender side reserved just for her.

On some level Levi must've loved her, too. She let that thought calm her mind and give her strength. She lifted her chin and cleared her throat. "That's my fiancé and his K-9 partner. They just got back from being stationed overseas."

His pause was almost as long as her own had been. "So, you've been…welcoming him home?"

The distortion app couldn't mask the sexual innuendo. "He was part of my life before you decided you needed to be my keeper."

She might have thought he'd hung up if it wasn't for the labored breathing that sounded like a weird sound effect from a horror movie with the voice distortion filter running. "I'm not happy about that. You belong to me, not anyone else."

"Well, you should have done your research better." She slapped her hand over her mouth as her response got ahead of the caution she usually used.

"I don't like your attitude this morning." The mechanized voice sharpened, and Zoe got the feeling *he* had put the phone right up against his lips. "I'm going to punish someone else on the list. Maybe your boyfriend. Or his dog."

"No. Please, I—"

"All those muscles won't stop a bullet to his brain or a truck speeding out of control. They didn't help your father."

Zoe fought against the emotions churning inside her. She needed to think like a criminalist. She needed to analyze what *he* was saying. She needed to figure out who this guy was, or her life would never be her own again. And she desperately wanted the life Levi and the baby promised. "You've never mentioned a gun before. Do you even own one? Ethan never used a gun to threaten or subdue his victims."

The gasp on the other end of the phone almost sounded like a real voice.

"That's right. I know you're not Ethan. Guns were never his MO. And if you're trying to copy him, you just made a mistake."

"I don't make mistakes." The mechanized tones returned, sounding colder and crueler than ever. "As much fun as this game has been, I think it may be time to punish *you*."

Zoe's hand immediately went to her baby. "What do you want?"

"Everything that's mine."

What did that even mean? Zoe shook her head. "What is it you want me to do?"

"I want you to die." Zoe's lungs locked up with a startled breath and she sank into her chair. "On my terms. On my timeline. Just like Ethan would."

She glanced at her ring again. Levi. Oh, how she wanted him with her right now.

But no. She needed to be stronger than that. She needed to be able to manage her anxiety so that she could take care of the baby and be a worthy, helpful partner to her future husband.

Zoe looked up at the clock on the wall and counted the

numbers, forcing her breathing to match every five ticks of the second hand.

There was a sharp knock at the door, and she yelped out loud.

Jackson Dobbs—six feet, four inches of taciturn co-worker—filled the open doorway. His icy gray eyes narrowed with an unspoken question. While she couldn't lie and say she was okay, she could hold up her cell phone and point to the caller everyone she worked with had now been warned about. He stepped into her office, his massive shoulders filling up the room much the same way Levi did.

Fortunately, Jackson wasn't one for long conversations. "Hang up and call your man."

"What's up?" she asked instead of immediately complying. "Please tell me we have work to do. I'd love to focus on that instead of…" Her gaze dropped back to her phone.

Jackson grunted a noise that she couldn't interpret. "Got a call. Female DB. Shallow grave. Discovered by cross-country skiers at Blue and Gray Park in eastern Jackson County. Witnesses freaked out because she's in relatively good shape. Dark hair. Not dressed for winter. Too frozen to have much decomp yet."

"She?"

"Yeah. ME will meet us there."

Zoe nodded and put the phone back to her ear. "You can finish your threats later. I have to go. I've been called to a crime scene."

"I heard. You be sure to do a good job," *he* warned. "I knew you'd eventually find Emily. Have fun."

Emily? Emily Hartman? Zoe had been chilled, but now her blood ran ice cold. She snapped her fingers, urging Jackson back into the room. "What do you know about my crime scene? Did you take someone because of me? Did you hurt her?"

"She was good practice."

"For what?"

"For you. Ethan will be so proud of me. I can't wait for you to find out all the details. I'll be watching."

He ended the call, and Zoe released the breath she'd been holding. She pushed to her feet and looked up at Jackson. "*He* says the DB is Emily Hartman."

Jackson didn't need her to explain the missing college student whose case they'd all been working on. "Call Callahan. Change out of that dress. Snow's pretty deep out there. I'll meet you at the CSI van."

Zoe closed and locked her office door before peeling off her beautiful sweater dress and carefully folding it back up into its sack. She pulled on her jeans and layered tops before tying on her fur-lined snow boots. Then she grabbed her coat and kit and headed out the door.

After shrugging into her coat, she pulled out her phone and texted Levi.

He called me. He knows you spent the night.

Instead of texting back, Levi called. She immediately picked up, needing to hear his voice. There were no hellos, just a "Did he threaten you?"

"He insulted your dog." She turned the corner and headed toward the garage where the CSI van was parked. "Of course he threatened me. And you. And Sky."

"Sky and I can handle it. Are you in a safe place? Can he get to you?"

She shrugged. "I'm heading out to a crime scene now. A suspected murder." She pushed through the doors into the open bay where the van was parked. Jackson sat in the driver's seat. He already had it running and warming up. "*He...he* sounded like *he* knows all about it. Like *he* knows who we're going to find."

Levi cursed. "Where? I'll meet you there."

"Not necessary. I'm partnered with Jackson Dobbs today." She opened the door to set her kit inside and climbed up into the passenger seat. "You know, the really big guy who says even less than I do? You met him the other day at the lab."

"Army vet? Petite wife?"

She looked over and up at Jackson's craggy face and imposing build. "That's the guy."

Her coworker's eyes narrowed for a second, wondering why she was talking about him. "I'll explain in a minute," she promised Levi before nodding to Jackson. "I'm good to go."

With a curt nod, Jackson pulled out of the garage into the dim, wintry sunshine.

Levi was still talking on the phone. "Tell him everything that bastard said so he knows exactly what's going on. You glue yourself to Dobbs until I can get there."

She cringed at the idea of adding more people to *his* hit list. "He has the sweetest wife and a baby at home. I don't want to get them involved—"

"Tell him. What's the address of your crime scene?" She heard Sky's excited woof and the staccato beat of paws and feet hurrying down the stairs. "I'm heading there with Sky."

"You'll be in the way."

"Damn right I will. Tell him." She heard the beep of his truck door unlocking, followed by an emphatic curse.

"Levi? Is everything okay?"

"Yeah. I'm on my way." He called to Sky again, and Zoe relaxed just a hair. She knew there was no stopping Levi from coming to her now. She hugged her arm around her belly, silently telling the baby how his daddy was on his way to protect them both. Levi's tone was softer when he spoke again. "I know you believe you're protecting everyone else by shouldering all this yourself. But I think that strategy is wrong. It keeps you isolated and vulnerable. Take away this guy's power. The more people who know you're dealing with this creep, the better. More people will have your back. It'll be harder to get to you."

"I think *he* killed this woman, Levi. *He* said she was practice. For me."

Levi cursed again, and she thought she heard rapid footsteps, as if he was running. "You go do your smarticle thing and find out who killed her. Let me watch your back so you can work. Then we can nail this bastard and get him out of our lives. Stick close to Dobbs until I get there."

"I will."

Jackson was really frowning now. "Still need a location, babe," Levi said.

"Blue and Gray Park. Somewhere along the cross-country skiing path. You'll see our van, plus the ME's. There'll be some black-and-whites there, too, blocking off access to protect the scene."

"Thank you. You still going to be able to get to the courthouse by three thirty?"

"I hope so. Depends on how involved the crime scene is. I'll have to finish my work there first."

"Understood. But we're doing this today, Zo. For the baby."

What should have been a promise made her feel a little sad. "For the baby."

After the call disconnected, Zoe leaned back in her seat with a heavy sigh. But Jackson had overheard enough to make him suspicious. "Are my wife and daughter in danger?"

Levi had that same ferociously protective look when he talked about their baby. He was going to make an excellent father. But Zoe wanted so much more. "If they don't have any contact with me, they should be fine."

He grunted. "Callahan joining us?"

She nodded. "He'll meet us there."

"Good. Until then I've got your back." He turned onto Highway 40 and drove toward the eastern edge of the county. "Congratulations on the baby, by the way. I wondered why you were wearing a lab coat that fits me. Callahan's a lucky guy."

It was the most words that Jackson had said to her at any one time that weren't related to an investigation. "I'm the lucky one. But thanks."

"Now talk to me, so I know what to expect at our crime scene."

It was time to go to work.

THE DEAD BODY was Emily Hartman.

"We're supposed to assume this is Ethan Wynn's handiwork?" Jackson speculated, looking down at the oddly preserved corpse. "Never did trust that guy."

"That's what that last phone call indicated." Zoe stood knee-deep in the snow beside the young woman's body while the medical examiner, Dr. Niall Watson, knelt beside the shallow grave that had barely been carved out of the frozen ground and covered with more snow than dirt. "But it's an impossibility. Ethan was already in prison when Emily was taken."

"We're looking at a copycat."

They weren't too far off the trailhead near the parking lot, so the collection of vehicles there was starting to grow as official vehicles and press vans arrived and the winter-sport enthusiasts out enjoying the trails on this cold, sunny day stayed out of curiosity to see what was going on. Yellow crime scene tape had been strung up between the trees surrounding the grave. A pair of uniformed officers worked on shoveling off the trail to transport the body to the ME's van, while another two officers kept the curious onlookers at a safe distance. The air was cold, but the day was clear, and Zoe could hear the buzz of numerous conversations as well as tires crunching over the gravel in the parking lot as people arrived or left.

But her focus was on the body in front of her. She and Jackson were waiting to collect soil samples and bag anything of interest at the site that wasn't part of the body itself. Other than some animal scavenging, which had dug up enough of the body for the skiers to see an arm and dark hair from the cross-country trail, the body was extraordinarily well-preserved. The body had been wrapped in plastic, which Dr. Watson pulled back to record his initial findings. If the poor young woman had been wearing leather skins and fur instead of jeans and a denim jacket, she could have been mistaken for an ancient burial victim dug up from the Ice Age.

Dr. Watson pointed a gloved finger at the cobweb of white lines on the victim's cheek before snapping a picture. "Those are ice crystals that formed within the skin. She was frozen hard someplace else and then moved here. I'm not seeing any blood or insect activity."

"Can you estimate time of death?" Jackson asked.

The ME shook his head. "Not while she's in this condition. But I'm guessing shortly after she was abducted. She's not malnourished. And I don't see restraint bruising on her wrists or ankles. Just petechiae around the eyes and the obvious markings around her neck." He pulled back the front of her jacket and pointed out the two tiny marks on the right side of her chest. "She was Tased. Probably how her attacker subdued her."

Jackson agreed. "Not much sign of a struggle at the abduction site."

The MO fit. Sort of. But something wasn't quite right about the evidence here. "Ethan used a Taser on Lexi's husband when he abducted her. But he used his fists and choking to subdue the women he killed." She swallowed hard. "He got off on the physical violence."

Dr. Watson covered the body again. "There are no indications that she was in a fight. No obvious defensive wounds.

I can't state conclusively until I do the autopsy, but I believe her death was pretty quick."

Zoe didn't think *quick* was in Ethan's vocabulary. He'd enjoyed toying with his victims—she herself was a case in point of the long game he liked to play with his victims before ultimately strangling them to death.

"*He* probably kept the body in a deep freeze somewhere. But now *he* wanted her to be found." Zoe was certain that was at least part of the meaning behind the cryptic comments in *his* phone call earlier. She huddled inside her coat, feeling the chill of being watched as much as she did the wintry temps. "Wait. Could I see her left hand?"

Dr. Watson reached inside the plastic and held up the appendage.

Zoe pointed to the indentation at the base of the victim's third finger. "She was wearing a ring that *he* took. I remember her mother mentioning it when we interviewed her. It was her grandmother's ring. Emily always wore it. *He* took a souvenir. Ethan kept pieces of jewelry from his victims."

"Good memory, Ms. Stockman." The ME tucked her hand back inside the plastic.

"*He's* copying Ethan. I bet *he's* here right now, watching. Maybe even taking pictures."

Zoe glanced over her shoulder to the gathering of people and vehicles beyond the crime scene tape, wondering if she'd see *him* looking right at her. Was *he* hidden inside one of the vehicles? Blending in with the crowd? Levi thought *he* was someone in her life. But she didn't see any familiar faces beyond the two men with her, the police officers and a couple of reporters she recognized from the television news. She also recognized Jordan Fletcher from his earlier push to document a crime from the moment the crime lab began an investigation to the hopeful conviction and sentencing at the end of a trial.

She also scanned the parking lot for Levi's truck, feeling a nervous anticipation, waiting for her Marine to arrive. Even with the distance between her and the crowd, she felt vulnerable, exposed. But Levi's presence would calm her anxiety, make her feel more secure out in the open like this. She knew he wasn't a hundred percent recovered from his ordeal in the Middle East and everything she'd put him through. But she was one hundred percent certain that she loved him. One hundred percent certain that he'd make a wonderful father. And one hundred percent determined to make their marriage into a real one if he'd give her the chance. She needed Levi in her life, his strength, his support. And as much as she was able, she wanted to give him that same strength and support in return.

"Zoe!" Jordan called out her name when her gaze moved past his, snapping a photograph the moment they locked eyes.

Zoe spun away and muttered beneath her breath at the man's persistence. "Earn your own Pulitzer and leave me out of it." But since he was staying on his side of the crime scene tape with the rest of the crowd, she couldn't very well have him removed from public property.

"He bothering you?" Jackson asked.

She shook her head. "I can't stop him from being annoying. It's just who he is. I was looking for Levi, and…" She waved aside that anxious train of thought and concentrated on the job she needed to do. "Let's just focus on processing the scene and get out of the spotlight as soon as we can."

Dr. Watson exchanged a curious look with Jackson before pushing to his feet. "You sure you're all right? You look pale."

"It's my natural look." She tried to joke. But neither man laughed. Although appreciative of their concern, she dismissed it. "I'm okay." She insisted. She *needed* to be okay. "Just ignore the reporter and keep working. That's what'll help me the most."

Jackson patted her shoulder. "Callahan will be here."

She nodded, and the ME got them all back to work. "Let's get her up on the gurney."

Zoe steadied the gurney as he and Jackson lifted Emily's body and put her, along with the plastic sheet she was wrapped in, in the body bag. They'd still have to get the victim from the grave site to the ME's van parked at the trailhead, but first the dark-haired doctor tucked everything thing carefully into the bag and started to zip it shut.

"Wait." Zoe stopped Dr. Watson with a hand on the sleeve of his coat and stepped up beside the gurney to take a closer look at the detail that was nagging at her subconscious.

She pointed to the band of bruising around her neck.

"That wasn't made with a curtain cord. That's how Ethan killed his victims. This is more like a thick strap of some kind…"

"Maybe the victim's backpack?" Jackson suggested.

"That was left at the crime scene." The strap of her camera tangled with the scarf around her neck, giving her an idea. She unwound the wool scarf looped around her neck and held it closer to the victim. "A scarf. Maybe not wool at the time of year she was taken, but a scarf." She looked up at Jackson. "We'll process any random fibers on her clothes and in the plastic. Maybe we can figure out what the killer used to strangle her."

"I'll get on that back at the lab." Jackson pointed inside the denim jacket. "Zoe."

He pulled his long tweezers out of his kit, and Zoe aimed her camera to document the photograph that had gotten lodged between Emily's body and the plastic tarp before he removed it. She opened an envelope to hold the photo but stopped when Jackson turned it over and she saw an all too familiar image.

"What the hell?" That was Dr. Watson.

Jackson cursed.

Zoe's stomach rolled as her own likeness stared up at

her. It was a picture of her at the original crime scene where Emily had been abducted. Why was there a picture of her from months earlier with today's dead body? Had *he* been following her for that long?

Dr. Watson voiced the logical question. "What do you have to do with Ms. Hartman's killer? Besides the physical resemblance between the two of you."

"Physical…?" Puffs of her breath clouded the air around Zoe's face as she gasped for air. Her hands instantly went to her belly at the panic rose inside her.

"Nice shot." She heard the click of the camera close by and whirled around to see Jordan Fletcher standing only a few feet away, at the edge of the crime scene tape. "Is it true? Is that Emily Hartman?"

She was also aware of every other reporter and curiosity-seeker zeroing in on Jordan's location and his conversation with her. *Breathe, two, three, four, five. Stay in the moment.* "What did you take a picture of?"

"You. Working a crime scene."

Just like the photograph she held in her hand. She quickly dropped it into the envelope out of sight. "This is evidence. You c-can't publish that."

She heard the pinging of flying gravel and the door slam on a vehicle and the murmur of voices started up again. Although thankfully not focused in her direction.

"Jordan Fletcher, *Kansas City Journal.*" He introduced himself to the two men who'd flanked her and helped block the crowd's view of the corpse. "That shot was pure gold. You holding a picture of yourself that was found on a murder victim?"

"Why are you taking pictures of her?" Jackson demanded.

Jordan glanced up at the big man beside her. "Because she's a lot prettier than you. It'll sell more papers."

"I don't want to be in the newspaper."

He snapped another picture and kept on talking as if she hadn't spoken. "Photogenic as ever. Zoe, what can you tell me about the case?"

"I can't comment."

"Will you at least confirm that it's Emily?" The other reporters closed ranks, looking for any tidbit of information. She looked away and counted her breaths. "Oh, come on. You know I've been following this case from the night she disappeared. This is my chance to complete this story. Getting the scoop on this will be my big break. Looks like it's your big break, too."

What big break was he talking about? She was content to do her job. It was challenging, meaningful work. At least, it had been before *he* wormed his way into her life and took over. "I'm working, Mr. Fletcher. Please let me do my job."

"Jordan, remember? We are long past *Mr. Fletcher*. Can you tell me how she was killed?"

"Her death is under investigation."

"You know it's murder." He pushed. "She hasn't been missing all this time and then finally shows up in the same clothes she was last seen in because she went for a walk and got lost. Besides, I heard you talking about strangulation. Is she another victim of Ethan Wynn's?"

Eavesdropping? Was he going to print that, too? Okay, now she was just getting angry. "Ethan is in prison."

"A copycat, then? You have to tell me something."

"No, she doesn't." A pair of broad shoulders and a black watch cap loomed up behind Jordan. "Sky, seek." The black-and-tan dog dutifully trotted beneath the crime scene tape and went straight to Zoe. He snuffled his nose against her coat, then sat and turned back to Levi as if to say he'd found what they were looking for. "Good boy. Stay with her."

"Stay, Sky," she echoed. Relief warmed her body like a mug of hot cocoa. Not only was Sky leaning against her leg and allowing her to pet the top of his head, but Levi was here, using the bulk of his coat and his own body to wrestle Jordan back a step and block his view of her and the crime scene.

"Hey. Hands off me, man." Jordan protested. "Freedom of the press and all that. This is *my* story to break. Get your own source."

"I'm not a reporter."

"Then back off and let me get my story."

"You back off."

When one of the uniformed officers stepped forward to intervene, Zoe caught the young man's attention. "He's with us—crime scene security. Master Sergeant Levi Callahan."

The young officer frowned, repeating Zoe's claim. But when he glanced at Jackson and Dr. Watson, both men backed up her claim that Levi was part of their team.

"The dog, too," Zoe added, burying her fingers into the thick fur above Sky's collar. Maybe getting a therapy dog would be a good antidote to her panic attacks—or maybe just knowing that she was taking control of this situation was what was helping her calm her pulse and regulate her breathing again.

"Yes, ma'am," the officer answered politely before asking Levi if he needed any assistance.

"The crime lab will make a statement when it's ready," Levi explained quite succinctly as he leaned into Jordan Fletcher's personal space, forcing the other man to retreat without ever laying a hand on him. He raised his volume so that everyone in the crowd could hear him. "There is no story to tell yet. They're still working."

"I have a relationship with Zoe. I've covered her work on Emily Hartman's case from day one." Jordan gestured in the air, as if reading the title on a marquee. "From Missing to Murder. Star of the Kansas City Crime Lab solves the case. I can make her famous. It'll be great PR for the crime lab."

Zoe clung to Sky's fur. "I don't want to be famous."

"I do." Jordan leaned around Levi's shoulder but didn't come any closer. "Come on, a serial killer returns to Kansas City? I break this story, I'll hit the big time. Is this Ethan Wynn's handiwork?"

"Ethan didn't kill her." Zoe was absolutely certain of that.

"But the MOs match. Do you think he's innocent of those other murders, too?"

"No."

"Did you and your lab put away an innocent man?"

"You're done." With a nod to the waiting officer, Levi had the reporter escorted away from the crime scene.

"I'm filing a complaint with the city. You're violating my first-amendment rights. This is all going into my article. Crime scene security, my ass." Jordan wrenched his arm free from the police officer's grasp and turned on Levi. "Who are you anyway?"

"Zoe's soon-to-be husband. You think you have a relationship with her? Think again. Now get out of her face so she can do her job."

But Jordan didn't know when to quit. He tried to make eye contact with Zoe and talk around him. "I saw that photograph in your hand. The one that was buried with the body? It's you, isn't it? A picture of you found with the dead body?" The crowd was buzzing again. It felt as if even Levi wouldn't be able to keep everyone under control. "Is Emily's murder connected to you? Are you the next victim, Zoe?"

Levi gave a shrill whistle between his teeth. "Sky, come!"

The dog immediately pushed to his feet and bounded to his partner's side. Levi whispered something else, and Sky bared his teeth and growled.

It was like a drop of water hitting an oily puddle. The moment Sky snarled, the crowd all backed away a step or more, including Jordan, who nearly tripped over his feet in his haste to retreat.

"Fine. I'm going. Call off your dog. I'm going."

Levi didn't wait to watch the uniformed officer escort Jordan Fletcher to his car. With a tap to his thigh and a heel command, he and Sky ducked beneath the crime scene tape. "Sorry it took me so long to get here. Your *friend*, or somebody *he* hired, slashed my tires."

"What?" Yet another casualty of this terror campaign. "I'm so sorry."

He looked so tall and strong and invincible as he waved aside her apology and closed the distance between them. "I called Aiden to take care of it. I upended your junk drawer to find your spare keys and drove Pinky here. *He's* going to know you're here because of the tracker, but I needed to get to you as soon as I could. You okay?"

Zoe walked right into his chest and hugged her arms around his waist, tucking the top of her head beneath his chin. "I'm just glad you're here. *He* knew I was coming here anyway. He's probably in the crowd someplace, watching. This is all some elaborate game he's been playing for months. The dead body is the missing-person case we've been working on." She shivered. "There was a picture of me buried with her."

Levi cursed and pulled away. "And that's our cue to leave." He pulled her camera from around her neck and tucked it inside her kit before latching it shut and picking it up. He turned to Jackson and Niall Watson, who'd gone back to the gurney to secure Emily's body. "You two okay finishing up here by yourself? We have a wedding to get to."

Jackson answered. "We've got this." Dr. Watson nodded his agreement.

Levi extended his arm to shake hands with Jackson and the ME. "Thanks, man. I owe you."

"No, you don't. She's one of the family." The compliment

from her coworker surprised her almost as the feel of Levi's hand slipping around hers and pulling her to his side. "Go put your ring on her finger."

Chapter Twelve

Zoe held her hair up while her dad fastened the pearl necklace behind her neck. She'd decided to wear her hair down, simply because she didn't have time to do much more than run a brush through the long strands. She and Levi had been late to the courthouse after stopping by the crime lab and her apartment. The judge had said he'd stay as late as five o'clock to marry them but wanted to get home for a son's basketball game.

So, no church, no wedding dress, no music, no time to fix her hair or put on makeup, no reception planned. Just barely time enough for them to duck into an office that was closed for the week between Christmas and New Year's.

Brian Stockman smoothed his hands across her shoulders and hugged her from behind when he'd finished. "Are you sure about this sweetheart? It's not the Dark Ages. You don't have to marry a man just because he knocks you up."

Zoe smiled at her dad's archaic words but appreciated his concern. She released her hair and reached up to squeeze his hand. "I'm sure, Dad. I want Levi to be a part of this baby's life."

Her father released her and slipped his arms back into the cuffs of his metal crutches before he hobbled around to face her. "He can do that without a wedding ring. I want you to marry the man who loves you the way I loved your mom."

Yeah, well, fate had decided her heart belonged to Levi

Callahan instead. "We care about each other, Dad." She reassured him. "And I believe he loves the baby as much as I do. Legally, it makes everything easier."

"Tell me you want to walk out of here, and I will take you home myself."

Her dad had always been a big man, tall and broad-shouldered. He'd been both father and mother to her for most of her life and her hero since she was a little girl. But he was slightly stooped now, thanks to the multiple surgeries on his legs and the supportive boot and leg brace he wore. And she could see more strands of gray in his thick, dark hair than he'd had before the accident that was no accident.

"I'm a lucky girl to have a dad like you." She dropped her hand to caress her belly. "I want your grandchild to know that same kind of paternal love. He or she will get it from Levi."

He pulled her in for one of the bear hugs she adored and dropped a kiss on the crown of her hair. "All I ever wanted was for you to be happy and safe."

She squeezed him back just as hard as she could. "Love you, Dad."

A knock on the office door interrupted the tender embrace. When she pulled away to open the door, Levi was there, looking tall and imposing and all kinds of manly and handsome in his dress-blues Marine Corps uniform. For a second, Zoe's breath caught, and her pulse rate kicked into a higher gear. But it had nothing to do with her anxiety. "Wow," she whispered, feeling the prickle of her sensitive nipples straining against her bra. "You clean up nice."

His gentleness and protective nature were the first things she'd noticed about him that fateful Fourth of July when they'd first met. But now it was hitting her full force just how much she'd loved him, how proud she was of his service and how lucky she was to have this good man interested in her. He'd made her feel normal, desirable and worthy of love. *He* and her emotional hang-ups had sidelined their relationship for a while. But Zoe vowed right then and there that she would do everything in her power to reclaim Levi's love. To be his lover again. His partner. His wife.

His green eyes seemed distracted by her mouth. He cupped the side of her face in his big, callused hand and gently stroked the pad of his thumb across her lips in a tugging caress she felt all the way down to the juncture of her thighs. Good grief! She'd read that being pregnant might make her hornier than usual, but she was about to combust right where she stood with just Levi's shoulders filling up her line of sight and his hand warming her chilled skin.

"Levi?" she whispered, wondering if he was just as transfixed by the moment as she was. She reached up and rested her hand beside the medals and ribbons decorating his chest. "Are you all right?"

"God, I wish this was real," he huffed out on a deep breath.

Zoe raised her left hand to cover his with her own. She turned her head to press a kiss to his palm. "It *is* real. Real baby. Real ring. Real vows."

He gave a barely perceptible nod and lifted her gaze to meet hers. "Real threat."

She was the one nodding this time. But emboldened to express her feelings in a way that this man made her feel safe to do, Zoe braced her hand against his chest and stretched up on tiptoe to press her lips against Levi's. It was a chaste kiss, gentle and soft because her man needed a little tender reassurance right now.

His lips moved against hers, and he tunneled his fingers into the hair at her nape, holding her against his mouth as he supped from her lips and took what he needed to believe that she was willingly making a commitment to him today. That she wasn't going to turn away from him again.

For Levi.

For the baby.

For herself.

For their future.

With a throaty groan that danced across her eardrums, Levi stroked her tongue across the seam of her lips and asked her to open for him. It was a request she willingly granted, parting her lips and leaning further into him so that their tongues could meet, and she could taste the minty toothpaste on his breath. Her thoughts swirled into a riot of sensations as he claimed her mouth. He hadn't had time to shave, and the light dusting of beard stubble tickled her lips. She breathed in the woodsy, masculine scent of his soap that clung to his skin. She felt the strong beat of his heart beneath her hand. Zoe reaped the benefits of Levi's need, and that slow burn of attraction she'd felt moments earlier morphed into an overwhelming fire.

Her father cleared his throat behind her. "Save that for the honeymoon."

But with a deep breath, Levi lifted his gaze to meet hers. "Sorry. Judge Livingston said he only had about fifteen minutes before he had to leave. We need to get this done. You still with me?"

Zoe nodded. "We'll be right there."

Brian turned to Levi. "I may be hobbled up now. But you hurt her, and I will come after you. Eventually."

"Dad—"

"No need, sir. I swear on my sergeant's stripes that I will not hurt your daughter, that I will do everything in my power to protect her and take good care of her and our baby."

Brian grunted. "I'd feel better if you said you were crazy in love with her and wanted to spend the rest of your life together. But I'll take that promise."

"Thank you, sir." Levi held out his hand. Brian sized him up for a moment, then shook hands.

"Go on. Get in there. It has always been a dream of mine

to walk my daughter down the aisle, and if all I can do is walk her across the hall into the judge's chambers, then that's what I'm going to do."

Levi looked back at her. She smiled. "I'll be there." She promised. "I won't ghost you this time. We're in this together."

He nodded. "Sky. Heel."

They'd barely stepped into the hallway when Lexi came shooting out of the judge's chambers. "Here. I almost forgot." She pushed a small bouquet of pink rosebuds into Zoe's hands and wrapped her arms around her neck to pull Zoe in for a hug. There were tears in her boss's eyes as she pulled away. "Welcome to the family. Now we really can become friends."

Zoe nodded her thanks. "I'd like that."

Aiden carried Rose in his arms as he came up behind Lexi. "Come on, sweetheart. The clock is ticking." He ushered Lexi back into the judge's chambers before smiling at Zoe and leaning in to kiss her cheek. "You look beautiful, Zo. Levi is a lucky man. And don't think for one second that he doesn't know that." Like her father, Aiden was wearing his KCPD dress uniform. Nodding to Brian, he backed across the hall. "Sir."

"Murph." Once they were alone in the hallway again, Brian adjusted himself over his crutches and held out his arm to her. "Still not too late to walk away, sweetheart."

"Not gonna happen, Dad." Zoe linked her arm through his and hugged herself to his side. "I messed up. I had a situation, and I didn't handle it well. Instead of making things better, I hurt Levi. So, yeah, we have some issues to deal with. But I really do love him. And I'm 99.9 percent sure he still loves me."

He leaned down and pressed a kiss to her temple. "Still gonna kick his ass if I have to."

ZOE WAS NOW officially a married woman. Little about today had been traditional. But still, somehow, it felt special. She hadn't panicked at any point, possibly because the group in attendance was small and familiar, the judge plainspoken and kind, and she'd held on to either her father or Levi the entire time. The ceremony had been brief and businesslike. But that kiss beforehand when she'd promised to stand by his side felt as much like a pledge to her as the plain gold band on her finger did.

But now she was struggling.

They'd all gone out to dinner, and Zoe knew the other patrons in the busy restaurant had noticed the size of their group and how they were dressed. Her father hobbled in on his crutches. Aiden carried a sleeping toddler. Levi looked like he'd just stepped out of a military ball. Lexi had clearly been crying. There was no way to hide Zoe's pregnancy in that sweater dress, and she hated to be the center of attention. So, she had started to second-guess her decision.

Why on earth would Levi ever give her a second chance? Of course, they had the baby to bond them together. But what about eighteen years down the road when their son or daughter went off to college or trade school? What would keep them together then? Could they even last eighteen years? Eighteen months? The baby kept swishing back and forth in her belly, perhaps feeling her rising anxiety. Maybe warning her to get out of her head before her breathing staggered and her blood pressure spiked?

"That's it." Levi's voice from the far end of the couch startled her.

"What? What's it?"

"You're holding your belly as if you're protecting the baby. I can count the number of breaths you take increasing each minute." He pushed to his feet, and Sky trotted over from his spot on the rug to rest his head on Zoe's knee. His soulful dark eyes studied her intently, and she smoothed his soft ears beneath her hand. "You need to get out of your head. I can hear you overthinking whatever's going on in that brain of yours all the way over here."

"That's what the baby just said." Levi frowned as if she'd spoken gibberish. "I mean that's what I imagined the baby was telling me."

"Sky's alerting to you. He must be picking up on something. He hears the change in your breathing, or you give off some kind of scent when your blood pressure rises."

"Maybe you startled him when you popped up like that."

"Then he would have alerted to me." Levi knelt in front of her, his big hand settling over hers on top of Sky's shoulder, binding the three of them together. "You're about to have an attack. He senses it. I sense it. I'm not going to let you have a panic attack on your wedding night. That's no way to celebrate."

She had been getting herself worked up without fully realizing it, though the warmth encompassing her hand and the soft, concerned look in Levi's expression was calming her. "Celebrate? Levi, I didn't think we'd be cruising the Mediterranean. We're watching TV. Relaxing. And that's fine."

He leaned in and pressed a gentle kiss to her forehead. "No, it's not. You're not relaxed. Get your boots back on and bundle up." He pulled out his cell phone as he stood and sent a text to someone. "I know you don't want to take any time off work. And you've been holed up in this apartment way longer than you should have been because of *him*." His phone lit up. He read the response and smiled before typing in a quick reply. He looked almost boyish in his excitement, and her curiosity pushed aside the anxiety creeping in on her. "We're going to have a honeymoon tonight, doing something just for us. Do you trust me?"

She stared at the hand he held out to her and was reminded of the caring, protective man who'd seen her stressing out at that Fourth of July celebration all those months ago. He'd rescued her, held her, talked with her for hours, made her laugh and loved her. Zoe laid her hand in his and let him pull her to her feet. "I trust you."

"Thank you." He led her over to the door where their boots and coats were stashed. "I'll go warm up my truck. Stay here with Sky until I come back and get you."

Zoe squeezed his hand, halting his excitement for a moment. "Are you sure it's all right to leave? *He's* probably watching my apartment right now. *He* hurt Dad the last time I disobeyed *him*. What if *he* comes after us?"

Levi squared off in front of her and cupped her shoulders. The boy who'd briefly appeared was gone. The man—the Marine—had returned. "Let *him* come. *He's* already going to be upset that we tied the knot. Let's take control of this game. If we defy *him*, maybe *he'll* make a mistake, and we can catch *him*. You need this." He slid his warm hands up the side of her neck to frame her jaw between them. "I. Will. Keep. You. Safe."

When he lowered his head toward hers, Zoe braced her hands against his chest and stretched up on tiptoe to meet his kiss. Her fingers curled into the front of his sweater to clutch at the skin and muscle underneath. His mouth moved over hers, gently claiming what she so willingly offered, chasing away every doubt with the heat of his touch and kiss. With just his lips and his hands touching her, Levi lit a flame that licked through her veins and warmed her from the inside out.

Zoe moaned in her throat and leaned into him, winding her arms around his waist, desperate to assuage the desire that made her nipples tighten almost painfully and liquid heat pool beneath her belly at the juncture of her thighs. The moment she brushed against the erection pushing at the zipper of his jeans, Levi ended the kiss with a needy groan of his own. He rested his forehead against hers for several moments, his breathing coming in jagged gasps just like hers.

"You're my kryptonite, woman," Levi rasped against her skin. "You're mine now. No one is going to take you from me. You or the baby."

Zoe nodded. His words might've been a little possessive and Neanderthalic, but she believed him, treasured them. "You're mine now, too, Levi," she whispered, vowing never to shut him out of her life again, even if she thought it was for his own good. He needed her to talk to him, to trust him, and she'd give him that. She just had to be patient. He'd believe in her—in them—again if she just gave him enough time to do so. She hoped.

She rested her chin on his chest and tilted her gaze up to his. "You mentioned something about a honeymoon?"

He dropped one more perfunctory kiss onto her lips, then stepped away to pull on his watch cap and grab his coat. "Bundle up, sweetheart. We're going on a road trip."

When she and Sky made it down to the truck with its brand-new tires that Levi had thoughtfully warmed up for her, he opened the door and bundled them quickly inside. "Do you mind if Sky sits between us?" Levi asked. "And maybe hunker down a bit?"

"To hide me?"

"At least until we get out of the neighborhood. I don't want to make *him* too suspicious if *he* is watching."

Zoe dutifully slouched in her seat and invited Sky to rest his front paws in her lap to sit and look out the window. Basically, nothing but the top of her stocking cap was visible, and it was about the same color as Levi's tan seats. "This good?"

Levi nodded his approval and stroked his hand along Sky's back. "It won't always be this way, I promise."

"I believe you." She petted the dog's chest, and he seemed pleased with all the attention. "I'm trying to be brave and stay positive." The giggle that tickled her throat felt like a foreign sound to her ears since it had been so long since she'd found humor in much of anything. "But I'm more curious about where we're going, who you texted back in the apartment and what you have planned."

Levi grinned and put both hands back on the wheel. "I've appealed to that scientific brain of yours, haven't I? You want answers."

"You're not telling me?"

"You'll figure out the clues soon enough."

He entertained her with silly clues, and she half-heartedly tried to guess their destination as he wove through traffic and turned onto Highway 40 heading east. But more than the mental distraction, she felt herself relaxing as they headed away from the lights and noise of the city. Homes and businesses grew scarce as the landscape changed into rolling hills frosted with several inches of undisturbed snow. They passed windbreaks of evergreen trees with snow-laden branches. Zoe could sit up straight now that Levi was certain they weren't being followed, and she enjoyed watching the peaceful rural scenery go by. The sun had set a couple hours earlier, but the moon was high and bright in the sky, so she could see outside as they drove along. She cracked her window open, and Sky immediately pushed his nose against the glass to inhale the scents of the countryside. Zoe tilted her nose, too, to inhale the crisp, chilly air.

And now they were pulling up to the front gates of K-9 Ranch. While Zoe had enjoyed their quiet drive in the country, she was excited to see the signs announcing the renowned rescue and training center for dogs. Security lights came on as they neared the gates and the sprawling white farmhouse, red barn and outbuildings beyond.

"You want to have some fun with Sky tonight?" Levi asked as he stopped beside a communications console near the gate and rolled down his window. He pushed the Call button and waited. "I might even let you throw a snowball at me."

"Oh, you're on," she teased, touched that he remembered how much she loved being out in the winter weather. Hugging her arms around Sky's neck, she pulled the big dog aside so that she could take in every road and tree and the grounds of the well-kept ranch. "I've heard of K-9 Ranch and all the good work they do with dogs." But there was only the porch light on at the house. "Are they expecting us?"

"Yeah. I made an appointment."

The radio on the communications box crackled with static. "That you, Callahan?" a man's voice asked.

Levi stuck his face out the window so that the camera could pick him up. "Yeah, it's me, Ben. You ready for us?"

"I'll buzz you in. Pull up by the barn."

After a moment, the gate swung open, and Levi drove his truck up a long gravel road toward the house. He turned toward a parking area near the barn and concrete block outbuildings she now realized were kennels. Sensor lights came on all along their path as they drove past them, and soon the entire driveway, parking area and outbuildings were illuminated with a bubble of light. Their arrival triggered a symphony of barking, and Sky sprang up onto all four paws to answer.

"Easy, boy." Levi parked the truck and held up his fist to warn the dog to stop barking inside the truck. Despite the distraction of all the other dogs, Sky dutifully sat. But his tongue lolled out the side of his muzzle and he panted with anticipation.

A man came down the stairs at the side of the barn with a coal-black German shepherd at his side. Now that the place was lit up, Zoe could see curtains at the windows above the main floor of the barn, and she guessed there was an apartment on the upper level. He had a long, dark blond beard and wore a camouflage jacket with a hoodie underneath it as well as a knit watch cap similar to the one Levi wore. Oddly, though, he wore only one glove.

She pulled her gaze from the man striding toward them to look at Levi. "You made an appointment for a training session here? Why? Sky is the best trained dog I know."

"You've been cooped up in your apartment for too long, letting *him* dictate how you lead your life. I know you love the snow and being outside. I wanted you to have some fun. It's my…honeymoon gift, since it's probably not safe to leave Missouri and take a trip somewhere."

Her smile faltered. "Is it safe to be *here*?"

"They're closed a couple of weeks for the holidays, so there won't be anyone here but us." He nodded toward the man in the camo jacket and held up his hand, asking him to give them a minute to finish their conversation. "I met Ben Hunter, the guy we're going to train with, at that veterans' support group I went to at St. Luke's. He made the offer, and I said yes."

"But what about…*him*? Will he come after your friend? Or the dogs here?"

"*He's* tracking your vehicle, not mine. I check for trackers every time I go somewhere just to make sure. My truck is clean, and your SUV is parked at your apartment complex. So, *he* should think you're home right now."

Something inside her still made her cautious. But she wanted to shout for joy at the evening Levi had set up for her. "I can really be outside in the fresh air without worrying about anyone taking a picture of me or calling to threaten me?"

"Ben said security here is top-notch. Even though the owner and her family are gone on vacation, he's a retired Delta Force soldier. He has a working K-9 partner, Rocky, with over twenty other dogs on the ranch. I can't imagine any place where you'd be more well-guarded."

Zoe leaned back in her seat and eyed the scary-looking man waiting a few feet away from the truck. He was close enough now that she could see the reason he wore no glove on his left hand—he had no left hand. Instead, the black shepherd's leash was tucked inside the triangular hook at the end of his left arm. Her heart squeezed in sympathy at his disability. But the piercing look in his blue eyes told her there was nothing to pity about the man. He was a veteran and part of Levi's PTSD support group. She suspected he shared many of the same traits Levi had—observant, protective, devoted to his K-9 partner. If Levi trusted him and thought she was safe here at K-9 Ranch, then she would, too. "And Mr. Hunter will let you use their facilities to keep Sky's skills sharp?"

Levi nodded. "I want you to learn the basics of dog handling, too. I want Sky to bond with you as well as me so he becomes the family protector, not just my sidekick. I don't know how many tricks this dog can learn, but he's already picking up when you're distressed. Maybe he can learn to warn you when you're about to have an attack. If for some reason I'm not there, he could calm you."

Zoe framed Sky's muzzle between her hands and looked into his dark eyes while she petted him. "You want to be my hero, too, Sky?"

"Yeah, he does." Levi petted his partner more vigorously, getting him excited to work, and Sky whined between them. "You ready to meet the other dogs, boy?" Sky danced in anticipation. "Let's do this."

Ben came forward to meet them as they climbed out of the truck. "Hey, Top. Glad you could make it."

The two men shook hands. "Thanks for opening up late for us."

"Not a problem." Sky and the black shepherd nosed around each other, then sat, as if familiar with each other's scents. And they probably were. Since Levi had taken Sky to the therapy group at St. Luke's, she imagined Ben had taken his dog, too. Before they could complete introductions, a tall, tan dog with black ears and a curling tail trotted out of the barn to meet them. "I got this, Rex. Go back inside with the goats where it's warm." Ben gave the big dog a stern look and a hand signal, and he went back into the barn. "Anatolian shepherd. Not much for people, but heck of a guard dog. He thinks he runs the place."

"He minds *you*." Zoe pointed out.

"Because he knows I'm the real top dog around here." He smiled at his confident assertion, and suddenly, the disabled veteran with the stern countenance didn't seem quite so intimidating. "I'm Ben Hunter. US Army, retired. My K-9 partner, Rocky."

"Zoe Stockman, er, Callahan. Zoe Callahan." She glanced up at Levi, wondering if he'd be upset that she'd forgotten she had a new last name.

Before any kind of panic or significant worry sank in, Levi reached for Zoe's hand and pulled her closer to his side. He leaned down and pressed a warm kiss to her cool cheek. "That's going to take some getting used to. For both of us."

She saw nothing but sincerity and caring in his soft green eyes, and Zoe nodded.

Just as soon as he'd reassured her, Ben spoke again. "So, tell me exactly what you hope to gain by signing up for lessons here at K-9 Ranch."

"Like we talked about after the meeting. Exercise for Sky. Keep his skills sharp. And I want Zoe comfortable with handling him, at least on a few basic commands."

Ben nodded. "All right. Let's get started. We'll run him through a few paces, tire him out a bit. Then we'll let your wife take over."

A door closed at the top of the stairs beside the barn, and a woman with long, dark curls sticking out beneath the stocking cap she wore hurried down to join them. "Hi." Her boots crunched across the snow, and she greeted them with a shy smile. "Welcome to K-9 Ranch."

Ben immediately curled his arm around her shoulders and

snugged her to his side. "I told you to stay inside where it's warm, Sweetcheeks."

"Yes, but if I help with your evening chores, then you'll be ready to turn in when your lesson is done." She smiled up at the grim-faced man. "And you know how cold I get waiting up there alone. I didn't even have Rocky to cuddle with."

"I know how to keep you warm." The hint of a smile behind his beard softened his entire countenance. He lowered his head to exchange a gentle kiss. "This is my wife, Maeve."

They all shook hands and exchanged greetings. "Are you thinking of adopting another dog?" Maeve asked Zoe.

"Oh, no. Sky is plenty of dog for us right now. I just…" She pulled her coat snug across her belly and caressed the bump there. "I'm pregnant. I want to make sure that Sky will be okay with the baby."

"Congratulations."

"Thanks."

Ben shifted his wife's gloved hand to the crook of his elbow. "It's all a matter of proper introductions, making sure he still gets the exercise and attention he needs. He'll need to learn that all three of you are his masters, and there shouldn't be any issues. We can teach you—and Sky—those skills. Even kids can learn commands. You should see Mrs. Caldwell's kids. They're practically professionals now."

"That sounds wonderful. Thanks."

Then the bearded man turned to Levi. "You ready to run Sky through his paces? I've got an obstacle course set up behind the barn I use with Rocky and some of the other working dogs. Burn off some energy before we put him to work."

"Sounds good." He glanced down at Zoe. "You okay hanging out over here for a while?"

Maeve brushed her hand across the top of Rocky's head as she stepped forward. "You can help me feed the kennel dogs.

And there's a litter of puppies in the barn I need to distract for a bit while Mama eats and gets some time outside to herself."

Zoe lit up at the other woman's invitation. "Puppies? You're speaking my language. Of course I'll help."

Levi squeezed her hand before releasing her. "Have fun."

"You, too."

"Sky, heel."

"Rocky, heel."

The two men and their dogs jogged out of sight around the barn.

"You two are sweet together," Maeve commented, inviting Zoe to follow her into the barn where she retrieved a wheelbarrow with a giant bag of dog food sitting in it. "How long have you two been married?"

"About three hours."

Maeve gasped, then grinned. "More congratulations! And I thought Ben and I were the newlyweds. We've been married a whole two months."

"Congratulations to you, too."

Maeve rolled the wheelbarrow out to the kennels, raising her voice above the din of barking dogs waiting for dinner. "Thanks. So, what are you doing here on your wedding night?"

"We can't exactly travel right now," Zoe answered, without really explaining anything. "I was getting a little stressed out over…things. Levi thought I could use a break." She glanced over her shoulder where she could hear the men shouting commands and putting the two German shepherds through exercises that sounded like they were all having fun. "Honestly, I think he can use the break, too. He's only been out of the Corps for a few days. He's still decompressing, I think."

Maeve opened the bag and handed Zoe a scoop. "Ben has serious PTSD. But he's doing so much better now. The therapy sessions help. And Rocky has been a godsend for him.

For me, too. They're the only reason I'm alive. Now I couldn't feel more safe or more loved."

It was on the tip of Zoe's crime-solving brain to ask the other woman for more details about whatever situation she had survived and find out how she'd been able to move on to the apparently happy life she was living now. But she worried she'd dredge up bad memories and dull Maeve's friendly smile.

Keeping her curiosity to herself, Zoe followed Maeve into the first enclosure and watched the other woman interact with a fearsome-looking pit bull mix who promptly rolled over onto his back for a tummy rub. Zoe added the scoop of kibble to the dog's dish, then allowed him to sniff her closed fist before he deemed that she was worthy of petting him, too. Even though the dog wanted more cuddles, Maeve shooed him back into his warm enclosure and closed the outer gate. "Finding their place in civilian life is a big challenge for men like them. Levi is lucky to have a partner like you who gets that. Who supports him. Who helps him get out of warrior mode to blow off some steam and be happy."

"I haven't always been a great partner," Zoe confessed, moving on to the next enclosure with Maeve.

"You are now. Letting him bring you here. Giving him time with something familiar. That man adores you. You can see it in the way he looks at you and the way he treats you. He loves you."

Zoe stopped, wondering how a woman she'd just met could see more clearly into their relationship than she could herself. "Yeah? I love him, too. Levi is the best thing that's ever happened to me."

Now she just had to convince him to trust that love—to trust her again. Maybe then their marriage could become the real thing and calling each other husband and wife would sound perfectly right.

Chapter Thirteen

Levi peeled off the T-shirt he slept in and reached for the scar ointment to massage into his damaged skin. He couldn't feel pain in some places anymore, as the burns had been deep enough to take out a few nerves. But in other places, he could feel the stiffness of the scar tissue and needed to keep the skin supple enough that it wouldn't impede his movement or cause him discomfort.

His nightly routine had been the same for weeks now: Shower. Brush his teeth. Apply the salve and bunk down in whatever solitary place he had to lay his head.

Not much of a wedding night, settling down onto the couch with a spare pillow and blanket by himself. But it wasn't the accommodations that frustrated him. He'd slept in a tent in the desert, a cot in the back office of the brig, in a jungle hammock and on the cold, hard ground with a log for a pillow. Clean cotton sheets on a couch that was long enough for him to lie down on felt like staying at the Ritz, by comparison.

He rubbed the ointment into the back of his neck, then twisted around to get the back of his shoulders and arms. He could hear Zoe getting ready for bed in her own bathroom and wondered if she was doing okay. The day had been long and stressful for her—for them both.

But the two hours they'd spent at K-9 Ranch had been

good for her. She'd been so tightly strung after the wedding and their dinner with family and friends, so afraid to do anything fun, anything for herself. So afraid of retaliation from *him* if *he* discovered that she was off living her life and wrestling with puppies in the barn and putting Sky through several basic commands. He even thought she might have made a new friend in Maeve Hunter.

To see her rosy, wind-whipped cheeks and hear her laughing as she threw snowballs for Sky to chase had done his soul good as well. Sky was usually all about the work, but a ball was a ball, and chasing it and claiming it was his happy place. Levi had laughed, too, to see the dog's surprise when he chomped on the snow and his icy toy vanished. It wasn't a traditional trip to Niagara Falls, but it was fun and meaningful and the best date he'd had in months.

He worried, though, that Zoe would revert to her fearful, closed-off self now that they were home.

Apparently, Sky was worried about her, too, because the dog kept pacing back and forth between his blanket by the sofa and Zoe's bedroom door. "Settle already, would you? You can't go in there to sleep in the comfy bed if I can't."

Sky's deep chest seemed to huff with resignation. The dog padded back over to his bed, turned around three times as if searching for the perfect spot to curl up in. Then he shot back down the hallway to greet Zoe and nuzzle her hand as she stepped out of her bedroom. Levi's baggy Marine Corps sweatshirt and the black leggings she wore weren't exactly a wedding-night-lingerie ensemble, but because it was his shirt on his wife and she was fresh from her shower and smiling, Levi thought she looked beautiful.

And beautiful he was not. Ignoring the jolt of longing that swept through him, he set down the salve and picked up his T-shirt to pull it back on. "Sorry. I thought you'd gone to bed."

"You don't have to cover yourself. We both have scars. I'm not afraid of yours." When he still pulled the shirt over his head, she went on. "They're badges of honor, Levi. Evidence of a career spent serving your country and keeping people safe. I couldn't be prouder of the man you are. They don't diminish what you look like. Not to me. Not in any way, shape or form."

"You're sure?"

"I'm sure. Now, who's my good boy?" He watched with a tad of jealousy as she petted Sky and talked to him in sweet, gentle nonsense words that the dog seemed to love. "My good boy, Sky."

"He's supposed to be a well-trained fighting machine," Levi pointed out, removing his shirt again. He hadn't realized how badly he needed to hear those words of acceptance. Out of all the things that made Zoe shut down and retreat from the world, it was a relief to know that his injuries weren't one of them. "Between your homemade treats and the snowball game, you're making him soft."

"I'm making a friend," she countered before her pretty blue eyes sought him out in the living room. "You really think I could take the Marine out of either one of you?"

Levi chuckled and squirted another dollop of ointment onto his fingers to try to reach between his shoulder blades and the small of his back. "Probably not."

She tapped her thigh and urged Sky to heel without the verbal command. Stopping to check the windows to make sure no one could see in told him that she hadn't completely forgotten that need to be on guard. Sky stayed right by her side as she circled around the couch to join him in the dim light of the living room lamp.

"*He* won't get you tonight, babe," Levi reassured her. "You're safe."

"I know. Thanks to you and Sky." She tucked a damp strand

of dark hair behind her ear. "But I've still got a lot of years of anxiety to overcome." When the needy gaze she gave him became too much to withstand, Levi turned back around and reached for the scar tissue he hadn't doctored yet.

Zoe turned her attention back to the dog. "Could you hear me in there, pacing? You're off duty now, big guy." She pointed to his blanket. "Sky, bed." The dog settled in at her command, and Levi thought she might head back to her room. But she surprised him by reaching over his shoulder and plucking the tube of ointment from his left hand. "Here. Let me." Her cool hands quickly warmed as she massaged the salve into the burn scars near the top of his back. He closed his eyes and reveled in her touch on his bare skin. "Either you're trying to become a contortionist or you need some help. How much should I put on?"

"Just a thin layer, rubbed into the skin as best you can."

"Like this?"

"Yeah." He leaned back into her massage, feeling her supple fingers working out the kinks of stress in the muscles beneath his damaged skin. "Perfect. Thanks." As she worked her way out across his shoulders, he asked, "Why were you pacing? You worried about something?"

"I was working up the nerve to come talk to you."

He broke off the massage and looked up at the woman standing behind him. "Working up the nerve? Zo, you know you can talk to me about anything." She tapped his shoulder, and he turned on the sofa cushion, facing away from her again. "Well, you used to know that."

"I remember. The best sleep I've had in years was when you'd hold me. And I wondered…" Her deep breath danced against his moistened skin, and goose bumps prickled across his neck and arms where the scar tissue hadn't taken away that ability. "Tonight was wonderful. But I don't want that to be a fluke. I want fun evenings like that to be normal for us.

To laugh and be happy. For me to forget about being afraid." Her hands paused their massage to clasp his shoulders from behind. "Do you think that we can have that one day?"

He hoped so. Instead of answering, though, he said, "Being with you calms me. Heals me."

"That's what you needed from me when you got hurt, wasn't it? To hear my voice?" She pushed her hands down the length of his arms. A strand of her damp hair fell forward and caught against the shell of his ear, and he shivered. The touch of her hair was cool, but the scent of her cinnamon-and-vanilla shampoo drifted to his nose, and he inhaled deeply.

Zoe was a feast for the senses—her touch, her scent, her gentle reassurances, her lush figure. His body instinctively reacted to that feast. Even that tiresome voice of caution guarding his heart couldn't stop his taut nipples from standing at attention or that most masculine part of him from hungering to be inside her again. He gritted his teeth against the erotic torture of her hands roaming his body. She doled out one more dollop of salve, then slid her hands against the scars at the small of his back.

When her fingertips dipped beneath the waistband of his sweats, he jerked. She immediately snatched her hands away. "I'm sorry. Did I hurt you?"

"No." Was that husky growl his own voice? "Your hands feel like heaven on my skin." He grasped one of her fists and gently pulled it open and laid her hand on his shoulder again. "Don't stop, babe. Unless what's happening here is freaking you out, please don't stop."

"I'm not freaking out, Levi." Perhaps misinterpreting the nature of his request, she began rubbing his shoulders again. "I bet you wanted me to get out of my head long enough to say that you are the strongest man I've ever known and that I believe you can get through anything. You probably needed me to tell you to do everything the doctors said, even if it was painful, so that you could come home to me. I'm sorry that you and Sky were hurt. But I'm even sorrier that someone you trusted, someone you cared about and were trying to help betrayed you."

"Are you talking about yourself? Or Ahmad?" That felt like a low blow. Her hands stilled on his shoulders. She was trying to mend fences, and his reaction to wanting her so badly, for caring so much was to say something crass to push her away. This woman's emotional bravery put him to shame. He turned on the sofa to face her, gently taking both her hands in his. "I'm sorry."

Her grasp tightened around his. "I didn't know he'd done that to you. I didn't understand that you felt I was doing the same thing. I'm the one who's sorry. I should have tried harder to be there for you. I should have told you I was pregnant. It would have given you a reason to fight to come home."

"I understand now why you pulled away from me. *He* didn't leave you any choice." He released her hands to pull her between his legs and push up the hem of her sweatshirt. Then he leaned forward to press a kiss to the precious swell of her belly. "You did what you had to do to protect our baby. Thank you."

Her hands came up to caress the back of his head, and he felt her lips rest against the crown of his hair. Oh, how he missed her gentle touches, how he craved them.

"Is this too little, too late?" she whispered. "Did we miss our chance?"

"No." He pushed her shirt farther up and rested his thumbs beneath the curve of her breasts. They were just as beautiful as he remembered—maybe more so now that they seemed heavier, fuller. He brushed his thumb across her dusky areola and nipple, and she gasped as her body instantly responded to his touch. "We're making our chance."

"What are you doing?" she asked, her voice a husky caress.

"What feels right." Levi scooted to the edge of the sofa, grasped Zoe's waist and pulled her between his legs, not caring if the arousal inside his sweatpants was nudging against her thigh. He touched his tongue to her sensitive nipple, and she groaned. "*You* were reason enough to come home."

With a husky gasp of his name, Zoe tipped his face up to hers and kissed him like she meant it. She nibbled on his bottom lip, then tugged it between her own, soothing the small nip with her tongue. When he demanded entrance into her mouth, her lips parted, and their tongues dueled. He heard the mewling sounds in her throat like strokes across his skin. And all the while, his hands were plumping, squeezing her breasts. Her nipples were teasing little spikes against his palms.

They made out like that for several minutes, lips colliding, hands exploring. His pulse thundered in his ears. He could feel her heart thumping beneath his fingertips. "Zoe…babe…" he whispered between kisses. "You were responsive before, but now… I need you."

"I'm yours, Levi. I always have been."

With the gift of those words, Levi pulled back. He wondered if his eyes were as fully dilated and dazed looking as hers. "May I make love to you?"

Although his arms had circled around her back to hold her, her hands never stopped moving—across his hair, the stubble of his beard, his shoulders and back to his face. "If you don't, I'm probably gonna have to hurt you."

He chuckled at her needy admission. "Yeah? And just how do you think…?"

Without another word, she peeled off her sweatshirt and straddled his lap. Even with the layers of clothing remaining between them, he could feel her core notched right against where he wanted her most.

A feast for his senses.

God, he loved this brave woman.

He needed her.

Levi lay back on the sofa with Zoe stretched out on top of him. "Maybe I should introduce myself to my son or daughter."

"I have a feeling our baby already knows who you are, Daddy."

"I missed you. So much." He raised his head to kiss her breasts, to nuzzle her neck.

"I know," she gasped. "Because I missed you just as much."

Their lips met again, and they peeled off any remaining clothes. And though the words of love never came, he showed her with his hands and mouth and body that she was precious to him, that he wanted her and how truly being together again would heal them both.

December 30...

No! SHE DIDN'T deserve a happily-ever-after!

Marriage and babies and solving murders. That wasn't supposed to be Zoe Stockmann's life.

"I control what happens to you. You're mine."

The photographer scrubbed the toothpaste over the ring, harder and harder, until scratches were being clawed into the skin surrounding the band of gold. Ethan Wynn liked his trinkets. He'd collected one from each of his victims—an earring, a necklace, a career-achievement pin. Ethan had kept them like trophies in a box, a fine little collection of all his cleverness and power.

The photographer was beginning to understand the need for mementoes. They were symbols of triumph, a tangible gift from the inferior victims who'd fought and lost. Ethan had been pleased with the family heirloom that Emily Hartman never would have surrendered if she was still alive.

The ring was for Ethan. But cleaning it, making it shine was for the photographer. The cheap, easy polishing technique was a trick Mother had taught. Someone might've questioned buying real polish or taking the ring to the jeweler's for a cleaning. But no one questioned anyone buying a tube of toothpaste.

When blood started to seep from the small wounds, the photographer stopped and ran cold water over the ring and the surrounding broken skin. After a quick dry with a dish towel, the photographer held the ring up to the morning sunlight coming through the window.

Lifting the ring drew attention to all the pictures strewn across the countertop. So many pictures, all of the same woman.

Zoe.

Pretty Zoe in her living-room window. Nervous Zoe in the parking lot, peeking around that ridiculous pink SUV. Focused Zoe at a crime scene, snapping her own photos and pointing out clues to the men around her. Happy Zoe, walking hand in hand with that bruiser Marine and his scary dog. She had no right to be happy.

Anger returned, and an idea formed.

When the photographer finally took control of Zoe, that sparkly engagement ring would be the souvenir. Ripped from her hand while she was unconscious. Maybe cut from her hand if she wouldn't cooperate.

The photographer had done everything just as Ethan Wynn had instructed.

This would be the big break.

This would please Ethan, give him exactly what he wanted. The photographer had learned from the best.

Breaking Zoe's spirit was no longer enough.

It was time to kill.

Time for one last picture, one last souvenir.

Then they both could have their happily-ever-after.

ZOE WOKE UP that morning and dared to think her life was better.

Her relationship with Levi had certainly changed. It wasn't just a reset to the relationship they'd shared that summer. She wasn't as emotionally exhausted as she'd felt the past several weeks because she'd finally gotten a full night's sleep—nightmare free, secure in Levi's arms. Yes, the sparks of attraction were definitely still there, as evidenced by the combustible way they'd come together on the sofa and again, later, in a gentler joining after he'd carried her to bed. And then she'd slept—the best sleep she'd had in months, secure in Levi's arms.

This morning was better because she felt hope.

She still had a tracker on her car. The text threats and phone-call recordings were still at the lab to be analyzed. There was still the body of a young woman with far too many personal ties to Zoe slowly thawing out in the morgue.

But with Levi in her life, at her side and now in her bed, she wasn't alone against the threat anymore. She still needed answers as to who was using Ethan's sadistic mind games and trying to copy his MO. But she could think more clearly this morning. She wasn't a hair's breadth away from suffering a panic attack just by waking up and worrying about what *he* had in store for her that day.

As she stood at the kitchen island, sipping her green tea and nibbling on the toast Levi had fixed for breakfast this morning, she was actually thinking into the future. She wasn't trapped in the past with her nightmares. She wasn't shutting out the world around her.

Okay, so she still hadn't opened her blinds and curtains for *him* to see her. There were still three locks on her door. But she'd kissed her husband and petted their dog before they left for their morning run and a perimeter sweep of the apartment complex and neighborhood. And now she was scrolling through a website on her laptop and jotting down items in her notebook she could buy for the baby or borrow from her brothers and sisters-in-law.

Handcrafted Missouri white-oak crib—wish list. Then she flipped to the next page and wrote under the *Abel/Tyler* heading, *High chair.*

She had moved on to another website and was reading through the pros and cons of different designs of rocking chairs when she heard a knock at her front door.

Zoe immediately tensed at the sound. Levi had his own key now. He wouldn't knock. Even if he'd forgotten it, he'd announce himself right away so she wouldn't be afraid. Whoever was out there knocked again.

Her hands began to shake. She fisted her fingers around her mug and set it down before she spilled any of her tea. Great. So much for starting a new day and thinking her life was better. It was irrational to think she could stop her anxiety issues just because she'd finally had a good night's sleep.

Oh, how she wished she had Sky's warmth leaning against her leg and his soft fur to cling to. She needed Levi's arms around her and his deep, gravelly voice talking her down from her panic.

She had to be stronger than this. "Come on, Zoe," she chided herself.

Emily Hartman needed her to be strong to solve her murder.

Her team at the lab needed her to be strong to do her part to get their work done.

Levi needed her to be strong.

The baby needed her.

"It's just a knock at the door," she told herself. "You don't even know who's out there yet." She pulled up the stopwatch on her phone and zeroed in on the numbers ticking by. *Deep breath in and count to five. Release breath. Five more. Breathe and count. Breathe.* Her visitor knocked again. "Just go look."

Keeping the phone in her hand and focusing on the numbers, Zoe walked to the door and peeked through the peephole. The moment her visitor noticed movement behind the door, she stepped back and waved. "Hi, neighbor. Got a minute before you head to work?"

Zoe exhaled a sigh of relief when she recognized the red ski suit and puffy earmuffs of her upstairs neighbor, Poppy Hunter. Zoe's fingers trembled as the adrenaline in her system abated. She unlocked the dead bolt and doorknob and cracked the door open to see what Poppy wanted. "Good morning. What...?"

The smiling woman pushed the door aside and swept into the apartment on a blast of cold, wintry air, carrying a present wrapped in pastel colors with a big yellow bow. "I told you I couldn't resist shopping for babies." Poppy went straight to the kitchen island and set the rectangular box on the countertop. She gestured to it with all the finesse of a game-show model revealing a prize. "Here's your first present. Go on. Open it."

Zoe closed the door after her. "Should I wait for Levi?"

Poppy pulled off her earmuffs and tucked them into her pocket. "Do men really care about stuff like this? I mean, have you ever seen one at a baby shower?"

"I think he does. The baby is very important to him." She drifted closer, curious to know what could be hidden inside the green-and-yellow teddy-bear wrap. It was a happy present, and she was as excited to see what Poppy had gotten for the baby as she had dreaded opening the brown paper package of moldy onesies.

Trying to hold on to her more positive mindset this morning, Zoe went to the island and inspected the package. It was heavier than she'd expected, so maybe it held something more than a cute outfit or blanket. Since she'd promised Levi that she'd include him in as much of the baby's life as she could, she set it back down to wait for him. She smiled over at Poppy. "Levi should be back any minute. Could I fix you a cup of tea or coffee?"

Poppy shook her head. "I can't stay too long. I've got a lot of things to do today."

"I understand." Maybe if she just went slowly enough, Levi would be back from his run before she had it all unwrapped. She paused to read the card attached to the bow and frowned. It had both Zoe's and Levi's full names on the tag: Stockman and Callahan. Poppy had seen the engagement ring, but she didn't know that they'd actually gotten married. Since her friend was kind enough to be excited for them, Zoe started to explain. "Actually, it's Callahan now. Yesterday, we—"

"Zo? Is everything okay?" The front door swung open. Levi's gaze immediately zeroed in on her.

"I'm fine," she assured him, crossing to him. She briefly squeezed his forearm before taking Sky's leash and unhooking the dog while he stomped off his boots on the mat.

"What did I tell you about keeping everything locked up?" He fastened the dead bolt behind him as Sky trotted straight into the kitchen and sat in front of the fridge, no doubt remembering that she kept the treats on top of the refrigerator. "Once I clean up, I'm going over to have another conversation with Gus. He was at his window, looking this way. If he's taking pictures again, I'm reporting…"

When Sky trotted past her, Poppy gasped and darted out of the kitchen, putting the width of the dining room table between her and the island. Before she could point out the visitor, Levi had pulled Zoe behind him. "That explains the door. We have company. Hey, Poppy."

He put out his arm to stop Zoe from moving around him

and glanced down at her, silently asking if she was all right having her friend here. She squeezed his arm again and gave him a quick nod, indicating that she was handling the visit okay. He relaxed a fraction, and Zoe hurried into the kitchen to get Sky his treat. She'd forgotten that Poppy wasn't a big fan of the dog. "Here you go, Sky. Good boy."

With Sky chowing down and plenty of distance between them, Poppy seemed her friendly, over-the-top, flirty self again. "Good morning, Master Sergeant."

He tucked his gloves into his running jacket and moved closer to the kitchen. "Just Levi is fine. Morning."

"Poppy brought us our first real baby gift." Zoe met him at the end of the island. "I thought we could open it together?"

"Sure." He rested his hand at the small of her back. "I'll let you do the honors."

Usually, Sky wolfed down his treat and then sidled up to Zoe to see if he could mooch another snack. But this time he didn't come back to her. He was sniffing around the kitchen, not settling. Was he on the track of the half-eaten plate of eggs in the sink she hadn't been able to finish?

But his nose didn't make mistakes. He put it to the tile floor and circled around the island. He must have detected the presence of their visitor. Interestingly, instead of approaching Poppy, he sat at the edge of the tiled floor and growled.

Poppy squeaked and darted behind a chair. "Zoe?"

Zoe clutched the sleeve of Levi's jacket. "Is he okay? Poppy, you don't have a steak on you by any chance?" She tried to joke. Growing more concerned about the threat to her friend, she released Levi and moved toward the dog. "Sky, come."

But Zoe hadn't gone three steps when Sky hurried over and sat in front of her. He actually sat on Zoe's foot and leaned against her, still growling.

She looked up to see a frown creasing the forehead above

Levi's narrowed eyes. "That's defensive behavior. He tried to stop me before the bomb went off. Maybe he doesn't like having a third party in the apartment."

"Bombs?" Poppy held up one gloved hand and cowered behind a dining room chair. "I certainly don't have a bomb. I'm sorry—that dog makes me really uncomfortable."

Levi retrieved Sky's leash and quickly hooked him up, pulling him to his side. "What's going on, boy?"

"He's probably picking up on how nervous I am around him." Poppy guessed. "Do you think you could get rid of him for a couple of minutes? Until I leave? Just until you open the present."

"And then you're going?"

Poppy cackled at Levi's question. "Thanks for making me feel so welcome. But yeah. I have errands to run. And I don't want to get attacked by Cujo there."

"All right. I can crate him for a few minutes. Sky, heel." Levi led his partner down the hall and opened the spare bedroom. Sky whined all the way down the hallway.

Suddenly, Zoe's thoughts pinged through her head with the speed of a rapid-fire machine gun. Her breathing went shallow and kicked into overdrive.

Sky's nose doesn't make mistakes.

He tried to save Levi.

He was trying to save me.

She hurried back to the kitchen island. She was in trouble. She'd seen the evidence.

The gift tag. It wasn't right.

Zoe Stockmann.

Two *n*s.

All of *his* messages to her had been misspelled.

It couldn't be a coincidence. This couldn't be true.

He was a she.

The gift was probably booby-trapped.

Her neighbor—her *friend*—knew a lot about Zoe's comings and goings. They chatted every day, at least greeted each other. Poppy had easy access to Zoe's SUV, her apartment, to her. She had no clue what the other woman's motive might've been. But all this time and she never even guessed that the enemy, her waking nightmare was so close to home.

What would Poppy do to Levi—to Sky—if she tried to warn them?

Zoe's hand went instinctively to her belly. Poppy had threatened her baby!

She picked up her pen and started jotting numbers in her notebook, visually counting each breath as she wrote, willing her panic not to steal away coherent thoughts. *Get out!* she wanted to yell. She needed to escape. No—she wanted Levi. She needed to tell him the person they'd been searching for was right here.

Her numbers became letters. As long as Poppy wasn't coming any closer, she could stay put. Stay safe. The other woman was actually moving away from her. Zoe frowned. That wasn't right.

Sky had sensed something was off about Poppy.

So, her neighbor had taken the dog out of the equation.

What was Poppy doing here? What did she want?

The panic was winning. Zoe had never claimed to have a poker face, and she didn't have one now. "Levi!"

She shouted the moment he reappeared in the hallway, pointing to Poppy. "*Him!*"

But her warning came too late. Levi never doubted her or hesitated. But even as he charged at the other woman, Poppy reached the hallway and fired the Taser she'd pulled from her pocket.

Zoe screamed as the prongs hit Levi in the stomach and

chest. He froze for a second. His hands shook. And her big, bad protector went down like a sack of bricks.

The moment Levi hit the floor, Sky's growling became a ferocious bark. Poppy looked up to make sure the door was secure before firing a second Taser shot into his back.

"Stop!" Zoe yelled, reaching for her purse and the phone inside.

Poppy calmly reloaded her stun gun and shot Levi a third time. His body convulsed, went still, and she smiled. "I'll save my last shot for that mutt, in case he gets free."

With trembling fingers, Zoe punched 9-1-1. But before the call could pick up, Poppy snatched it from her hand and carried it to the sink. She dropped it into the garbage disposal and flipped on the switch. The horrible cracking and grinding noises drowned out Sky's barking.

"Where are your keys?" she demanded, after flipping off the switch. Zoe glanced at her bag. Aiming the Taser at her now, Poppy went to the stove. "Get your keys. You'll drive."

"Please don't zap me with that." She begged, digging into her purse. "I don't know how the electric shock would affect the baby."

"Relax." Poppy pulled a knife from the magnetic strip near the stove. "I need you awake for now. I'm not dragging your ass to where we're going."

"Where is that?"

"Back to the scene of the crime. You're driving so I can keep an eye on you."

"Scene of the crime? You mean Blue and Gray Park?"

"Emily Hartman was a trial run. I made some mistakes. But I know exactly what I'm doing now. I hid her body too well the first time. Changed my mind." She hurried back down the hallway. "Stand by the door and don't try anything."

Poppy went back to Levi and fired the last shot of her

Taser into him. Zoe knew from her work in the lab that being stunned wouldn't render a person unconscious. But it could be extremely disorienting, he'd have no control of his muscles and the repeated jolts had to be causing Levi excruciating pain, possibly even paralysis. The attack would keep him down a little while longer.

She wanted to scream at the woman to stop. Levi had already endured more than his fair share of pain. But while Poppy zapped him, Zoe jotted a quick note below the list of baby items. *B&G P. Pinky. LU.*

Then she dashed to the door to retrieve her coat.

"You won't need that." The other woman had to raise her voice to be heard over Sky's furious barking. Zoe wondered if the dog was smart enough to unhook the latch on his crate and turn a doorknob.

"Could I at least check to make sure Levi is okay?" She needed to stall for time. Time her protector would need to regain control of his body. "I've never seen him so still."

"No!" She'd tried to walk a wide berth around the other woman, but Poppy slashed at her with the knife. "I said move!"

Fire tore through Zoe's side as the blade sliced through her clothes and left a gash in her side. She immediately pressed her hand against the wound. "You cut me!"

Poppy pressed the tip of the blade into her side again, leaving another, smaller wound. "I'll cut deeper, and closer to the baby, if you don't do exactly what I tell you."

Zoe felt the haze of panic swirl across her vision, but she ruthlessly shook it aside. She couldn't shut down. She had to function to protect the baby, to help Levi, to save herself. She backed away from the woman and the knife. "Poppy, please…"

She spun and grabbed the island counter, purposely leaving a bloody handprint on the corner of her notebook. Hopefully,

Levi or the police would see it like a bright red arrow point to where she suspected Poppy was taking her.

Blue and Gray Park, the scene of the crime where Emily Hartman's body and the picture of Zoe had been found. At the very least, since she was supposed to drive, she knew they'd be taking her pink SUV. Someone could surely track that.

"Move!" the woman screamed. Zoe felt a sharp prick near the small of her back and knew Poppy had stuck her with the knife again. With one hand still clutching the gash in her side, Zoe raised her other hand in surrender and opened the door. "We're going for a ride. You're driving."

The blast of cold air actually took Zoe out of her head for a moment. Her thoughts cleared and her breathing slowed as she inhaled a deep breath of winter. She grabbed the railing more than once, leaving as much of a trail as she could as she led the way to the parking lot. She pointed her key at the SUV to unlock it and start the engine so that the heater could warm it up. The cold air might be reviving, but no way was she dressed for a trek through the wilderness in the freezing temperatures. "You want me to drive to where Emily's body was found, don't you? Blue and Gray Park?"

She finally got a reprieve from the small pokes of the knife in her side and back as she climbed in behind the wheel and buckled herself in. She glanced up at the second-floor landing, blinking back tears of worry and fear when she saw no sign of Levi breaking down the door and Sky charging to her rescue.

Zoe considered several escape scenarios: Stepping on the gas and hoping Pinky would jump the curb and run over Poppy. Driving fast and slamming on the brakes, hoping the other woman would sling forward, hit her head and knock herself out. Even diving out of the moving SUV and letting Poppy crash was an option. But the risk to the baby was too great for any of those possibilities.

Poppy was smiling when she climbed into the passenger side. "That's right. The scene of the crime. Everything is ready for you." As if she suspected what Zoe had been thinking, she immediately poked her in the side of her torso. "Drive."

"I'm going." Zoe gasped and shifted into reverse. Other than the gash on her left side that would probably need stitches, she didn't think any of the knife wounds were life threatening. But they hurt, and the thought of how much worse they could get was shooting her adrenaline through the roof.

Meanwhile, Poppy settled in and started talking as if they were two friends going for a pleasant morning drive. She tucked the empty Taser into the pocket of her jacket and donned those oversized earmuffs. "I've done everything Ethan asked of me. Sent him pictures, turned you into a useless shut-in, killed for him."

Zoe frowned. "Ethan Wynn?"

"I was the perfect student. I'll give him everything you couldn't. Or wouldn't. A family. Love. An alibi for Emily's murder. I followed his MO to the letter. It will certainly cast doubt on his conviction of the other murders. The judge will have to release him, and we'll be together."

This woman she'd thought was a friend had clearly lost touch with reality if she thought Ethan cared about anyone other than himself and his obsession with controlling people. "Have you even met Ethan?"

But the knife pricking shallow cuts into her side and back was all too real. "I know him intimately. We write each other every week. Share our innermost thoughts and fantasies. I've visited him in Jefferson City. He wants love, a woman and a family, like any other man."

"He's using you. He uses everyone. He doesn't love you."

"Shut up!" The knife in her side cut a little deeper this time.

The truth wasn't going to sway Poppy from her mission. "Stop stabbing me. Please. Don't hurt my baby."

They sped toward the edge of the city. As they entered the countryside that she'd thought was so beautiful only yesterday, but now simply looked remote and far away from anyone who could help her, Zoe fought off the panic that threatened to leave her helpless. "Why are you doing this?"

"Because it's time for my happily-ever-after."

Chapter Fourteen

10 minutes missing...

"It's a pink SUV, Aiden! How many of those can there be in KC?"

Levi was down in the parking lot with Sky, on his phone with his brother-in-law and best friend at KCPD. When his nerves and muscles had finally started to cooperate and he could stagger to his feet, he opened the spare bedroom door and released Sky from his crate. The dog had immediately charged out to the kitchen, then run through the whole apartment, seeking out the woman Levi already knew wasn't there. Once again, the dog had sensed the danger, even when Levi's human brain had tried to convince himself that Zoe's friend was no threat to them. Levi had no clue if Sky could smell the Taser or some other weapon Poppy had on her or if he simply had a knack for identifying the enemy.

"A BOLO for her vehicle just went out. Give it time. Meanwhile, you need to see a doctor." Aiden insisted. "Getting shocked that many times can't be good for you. You were in the hospital just a couple of months ago. Let me handle this."

"Negative. I'm in fighting shape," Levi argued, turning 360 degrees, desperately looking for any kind of lead as to where Poppy had taken Zoe. "I messed up," he confessed, his heart feeling as rotten and bruised as the rest of him did. "I should have listened to the damn dog. He's right every time. I thought he was just being super protective of Zoe, not liking a stranger in the apartment. But he knew something was wrong."

The dog was dancing all around the empty parking space where a few drops of blood in the snow had replaced Zoe's pink SUV. It had been easy to track Zoe to this spot, but they'd clearly driven away.

She had her. There was no more *he*. Whatever sick game the crazy lady upstairs was playing, Zoe was gone.

But Aiden was being the best friend and the voice of reason right now. "Fine. You're on the scene. We could use your help. First, take a deep breath. Get that anger out of your head so you can focus. You're no good to me, or Zoe, if you're a loose cannon. Second, if your timeline checks out, they haven't been gone that long. They can't have gotten far."

"It doesn't take that long to kill somebody. What if she's already…?" Levi's deep sob was a silent gasp in his throat. "I love her, Aiden. She's my wife. Last night…we got to a really good place again. Forgave each other. Made promises to do better by each other. Now she's gone."

"I've got black-and-whites and Lexi's team rolling to your location." He vaguely heard his brother-in-law moving in the background. He and his K-9 partner, Blue, often rolled with the crime lab when they needed extra protection at a crime scene. "Zoe needs you to have your head in the game. She needs the Marine right now. Understood?"

Levi inhaled a deep breath. "Understood."

"Levi Callahan! Levi Callahan!" Gus Packard came running down the stairs and across the parking lot with his camera in his hands.

"Hold on a sec, Aiden. I need to deal with the neighbor kid." Levi tightened his hold on Sky's leash and sat the dog beside him. "Now's not a good time, Gus."

"You said to tell you if I saw anything suspicious." Gus

skidded to a stop just a few feet away, his gaze on Sky for several seconds before holding up his camera and turning it around to show him the screen. "I saw something suspicious."

Gus scrolled through the pictures he'd recorded. Zoe and Poppy coming out of the apartment. Zoe holding her side as blood seeped from her wound. Poppy forcing Zoe into the SUV. Zoe backing out of the parking space, her hands in a white-knuckled grip around the steering wheel. Zoe talking, probably trying to reason with an unreasonable kidnapper. Zoe angling away from her passenger as the blonde woman stabbed at her with a long-bladed knife.

Levi cursed. "You've got the whole abduction on your camera."

Gus looked as distressed as Levi felt. "Zoe's hurt. She was bleeding, and the mean lady hurt her with the knife. I don't like Poppy."

"I don't, either, Gus."

"Hey, kid!" Aiden yelled from Levi's phone.

"Your phone's talking to me," Gus said.

Levi switched it onto speaker. "Aiden is my friend. He's a cop with KCPD," he quickly explained. "This is our neighbor, Gus Packard. What do you need, Aiden?"

"I need him to print those pictures off for us. We'll use them as evidence."

"I can do that." Gus nodded, apparently liking that the police wanted his help. "I like to help my friends. One day Sky will be my friend, too, and I can pet him."

Before Gus went off on a tangent about dogs, Levi reached out and squeezed the young man's shoulder. "Sky and I are going to find Zoe. Did you see which way they went when they left the parking lot?"

Gus pointed. "They turned right."

Toward suburbs and countryside and the rest of the entire state.

How the hell was he ever going to find her? Before it was too late?

Wait.

He glanced back up at her apartment door. He replayed the last few things he'd seen and heard, when his brain had been too scrambled with the after-effects of multiple electric shocks. Now those observations were like puzzle pieces falling into place.

Even though he hadn't been rendered unconscious, the effects of being Tased had scrambled his brain a bit. He'd heard everything Poppy and Zoe had said, but those few seconds made it hard to process the details of what had happened. Zoe had said things out loud, giving him clues.

Sky had braced his front paws on the edge of the island countertop and nosed around it frantically until he'd knocked Zoe's omnipresent notebook to the floor. Levi had quickly picked it up, then nearly tossed his cookies when he saw the bloody handprint on one page.

A bloody handprint confirming the words he hadn't been able to understand.

Levi released his grip on the young man and patted his shoulder. "Good job, Gus. You gave me the clue I needed."

"I did?"

"Yeah. I think I know where to find Zoe."

"Sweet."

Levi was already tugging Sky along with him to his pickup truck. "You go back up to your apartment, Gus, and print those pictures. The police are coming to help. I need you to stay out of their way. But if you see anything else suspicious, you take a picture of it and you let me know."

"Okay. I can help." He turned and jogged back to his apartment building. "Zoe will like that I helped."

"Yeah, she will, buddy. Sky and I will, too. Thanks!"

Levi and Sky ran the last few steps to his truck and climbed in. He'd already broken down the door to Poppy's apartment on the third floor. But honestly, it was such a mess of photographs and letters and trash and more that once he and Sky had cleared the apartment with no sign of either woman, he'd shut the door and called his sister, warning her that there'd be plenty of evidence for her team to process.

He remembered picking up Zoe's notebook, seeing her efforts to stave off a panic attack. At the time, he'd thought that was what the letters meant, too, that they were part of her mental process after several rows of numbers. But now he realized her blood had been pointing them out like a red flag.

B&G P. Pinky. LU.

"Blue and Gray Park, Aiden. They're headed there in her SUV. I'm hanging up. I'll meet you there." Zoe needed his help. She'd said that out loud, too. But his brain had been such a scramble after those repeated shocks that they hadn't registered. But he understood now.

He spun up snow and slush from beneath his tires as he sped out onto the street and headed east.

Zoe hadn't shut him out. She wasn't trying to handle the threat on her own.

She needed him. She'd reached out to him.

He didn't intend to let her down.

Levi and Sky raced toward Blue and Gray Park.

"Love you, too, babe. Hang on."

30 minutes missing...

CIVIL WAR TRAIL was little more than a horse-riding path through the dark brown oaks and hickory trees of Blue and Gray Park. Zoe wasn't a great judge of distance, especially when everything was covered in snow, but she figured they'd already hiked about a mile and a half from the parking lot.

And now another shallow stab to her torso had turned her onto a knee-deep path through the trees themselves.

Even though the trees had lost their leaves, there were enough of them that it was difficult to see very far ahead of her, or to either side, as they zigzagged between them, and Zoe had lost her sense of direction. The sun was weak in the overcast sky and she was cold and shivering. She tried to keep her fingers warm by tugging down the sleeves of her sweater. But her boots and socks were wet, and her toes were frozen. She wasn't losing a lot of blood, but she was losing enough from the multiple stab wounds to feel a little light-headed. She'd already stumbled twice. But Poppy and her knife and her cold, smiling face kept Zoe moving forward.

"You're s-sure you know w-where you're g-going?" she asked, her words stuttering as her teeth chattered. She prayed Levi was all right. That he was awake and functioning. That she'd left enough of a clue that he'd be able to figure out where Poppy had taken her, and that he figured it out fast.

She hoped he was as good an MP as she believed him to be. *Find us*, she prayed silently, hugging her arm around her belly and the life she carried inside. *Daddy's coming for us, little one. He'll save us.*

"Up there."

One last poke of the knife pulled Zoe from her thoughts.

They'd reached a frozen creek and climbed up the opposite bank when she saw just how thorough Poppy's preparations for her had been.

Poppy had already dug a shallow grave, much like the one she'd put Emily Hartman's body in. There was a tripod set up at one end, and the hole itself was lined with a giant sheet of plastic. A long-handled shovel was stuck in the pile of snow and dirt beside the grave. Next to the camera was a small red gym bag.

Zoe wondered, ironically, about what was apparently Poppy's

signature color and why no one had noticed the bright red bag on the snowy landscape. Then she turned and glanced behind her. The grave was far enough below the lip of the creek bank that no one would see the red bag from the path.

No one could see the grave and the unfortunate soul buried in it, either, unless they wandered off the trail. Unless Poppy intended to leave a trail of some kind after Zoe was dead.

"Don't move," Poppy ordered. She unzipped the red bag and pulled out several items: A camera that she attached to the tripod. A scarf that criminalist Zoe would love to bag and test to see if there was DNA that matched Emily Hartman on it, but that anxious, kidnapped Zoe could only stare at and wonder what it would feel like to be choked to death. Next, she pulled out a baby blanket. What the hell?

Zoe stood there, shivering, fighting to keep her brain functioning even as her body was growing numb from the cold. "If you're trying to copy Ethan, you're doing it wrong. He never used a ligature like that to strangle his victims. It was always a curtain cord."

"Shut up! Emily wouldn't stay down when I Tased her. I had to kill her before I could move her. I was wearing the scarf around my neck. Subdued her that way." A weapon of opportunity. "I even used it to drag her to the freezer in my storage unit. A curtain cord would have cut into my hands."

Please let me live through this. Please let me find the evidence to back up every little detail she's confessing to me.

The next thing Poppy pulled from the bag was a box. She opened it and pulled out two cartridges to load into her Taser.

"H-he never used a T-Taser, either. He was s-strong enough to overpower the women he kidnapped."

"Well, I'm not." Poppy pushed to her feet and aimed the Taser at Zoe. "Ethan loves me anyway. I'm going to show him that I killed you. Then I'm going to take your baby and we'll be a family, and we'll live happily-ever-after."

Poppy fired the weapon. The prongs hit Zoe square in the chest, and a jolt of electricity arced between them, filling her with pain and momentarily stopping her breath. Zoe crumpled to the snow and rolled down into the grave. She landed flat on her back in the middle of the plastic. From her vantage point, she could see the trees and gray sky above her.

Even though she couldn't make her hands or legs or any part of her body immediately react, her brain continued to process what was going on around her.

Poppy set down the Taser and picked up the scarf, winding it around one hand. She adjusted the camera so it was focused down on Zoe and snapped several pictures. Then she did something else to it, setting a timer or starting a video recording, Zoe guessed, before Poppy stepped down into the grave and looped the scarf around Zoe's neck.

Maybe if Poppy hadn't stopped to smile up at the camera and say "This one's for you, darling," she would have realized just how quickly Zoe was recovering from the Taser attack.

The woman had terrorized her for months.

She pretended to be her friend yet had played on Zoe's anxiety and nightmare relationship with Ethan Wynn.

She'd planned Zoe's murder, right down to getting Levi and Sky out of the way. She'd hurt the man Zoe loved.

This woman had threatened to take her baby!

The scarf was just beginning to tighten when Zoe reached up and grabbed the shovel. The angle was awkward, her fingers were stiff, but she was smart and motivated and so angry that this woman would threaten her baby that she grabbed the handle and simply yanked it down. The handle cracked Poppy over the head, startling her enough to loosen her grip on the scarf. Zoe tugged at the silk and pulled it free.

Then, instead of fighting her for the shovel, Poppy climbed out of the grave and ran for her bag. Zoe rolled and pushed to her feet. Her balance was a little wobbly, but she could get a better grip on the handle. She swung it back like a baseball bat just as Poppy rose with the Taser in her hand.

"Ethan wants you to die! I want my happily—"

Zoe heard something akin to the thundering of hooves charging through the trees. She heard a vicious snarl and turned to see Sky scramble over the edge of the creek bank and leap at Poppy.

He knocked Poppy into the snow, and she screamed. Sky's long muzzle clamped around her arm, but she still had the Taser in her other hand. When Poppy pointed the weapon at Sky's chest, Zoe didn't hesitate. She swung the shovel and brought it down hard on Poppy's arm, knocking the weapon beyond her reach.

She raised the shovel to hit her again, but strong arms circled her from behind.

"It's okay, babe." She didn't need to hear Levi's voice to know that he was here. She recognized his arms, his strength, his scent. He pried the shovel from her hands. "Sorry we're late. But we're here. She's down. You're safe." He jammed the shovel into the snow again and stepped out of the shallow grave, lifting Zoe with him. "Sky! Break!" The dog released his hold on Poppy but only briefly glanced at Levi before growling at the woman again. "Guard!" Levi ordered.

Sky was panting from what must have been a hard run even before he'd gone after Poppy. But he sat right beside her, his head hanging over her like a vulture focused on his next meal.

Poppy whimpered and hugged both arms to her chest. She was bleeding from where Sky had chomped on her arm, and two of the fingers on her right hand were bent at an unnatural angle. Zoe must have broken them.

"Good boy, Sky." She praised the dog even as she leaned back into Levi's body. "You are so getting a new batch of treats when I get home."

"Get him away from me." Poppy begged. "I really do hate dogs."

"I love them," Zoe replied, feeling the last shot of adrenaline working through her system. "And he's not going anywhere. You could have hurt my baby. You threaten my child again, and I will sic this dog on you again." She turned her head and tilted her gaze toward Levi. "I can do that, can't I? Sky will go after somebody if you tell him to?"

He grinned. "Oh, yeah."

Zoe heard more footsteps, and suddenly Aiden Murphy and his dog, Blue, along with several other uniformed officers appeared over the top of the creek bank.

Aiden shook his head. "Looks like we missed all the fun. Levi, you want to call your dog off so we can cuff her?"

"Not especially."

Zoe chuckled at Levi's deadpan delivery.

"That woman terrorized my wife, kidnapped her, tried to kill her—"

"Murdered Emily Hartman," she added.

"Attacked me."

"Oh, and she tried to hurt Sky."

Aiden shook his head, but he was grinning, too. "We'll start with those charges. There's an ambulance waiting in the parking lot. We'll see if any of her injuries are life threatening. If not, we'll put her in the back of my squad car and book her."

Poppy tried to shimmy away. Sky growled. "Put me in the police car. Now."

Zoe pushed against Levi's supporting arm. "You're scared of this dog?" Poppy nodded. "Good. You should be. You should be scared of me, too, because I have hormones and emotions raging through my body, and I can't take anything for them." Then she turned and stumbled into Levi's embrace. "I want to go home."

He scooped her up into his arms. "Ambulance first, babe. I know she cut you."

"Okay." She waved at Aiden. "Don't move anything until the lab gets here to process the evidence." She pointed to the camera that was probably still running. "Oh, and most of what happened here today is on film."

"Got it, Zoe. I'll call Lexi." He winked. "You did good."

"Thanks." Then she settled into Levi's embrace. "I'm crashing. No more energy. And I'm so cold."

"I've got you, babe. Take off my watch cap and put it on. That'll help warm you up. Tuck your hands inside my jacket." She did as he instructed, feeling warmer and safer already. "Sky, heel." The dog moved right along beside his partner, no leash needed, as he exchanged a nod with Aiden and carried her down the creek bank. "I want both of you checked out. I really don't like seeing blood on you. You may need stitches."

"Okay. The baby's fine. I protected him."

"I know you did, Mama. Thank you for that."

"Are you okay?" she asked. "I never wanted anyone else to get hurt."

"I know that. And I'm fine. So, don't you worry. I don't need you to have a panic attack right now."

"I won't." She promised. "Because you're with me."

He pressed a kiss to her temple. His long, powerful strides quickly took them back to the marked trail and out to the ambulance. "I want them to admit you to the hospital, make sure there's no frostbite or risk of infection from those cuts or harm to the baby."

"Okay."

"Then as soon as you're released, I'm going to bring you home and take you to bed where I can hold you in my arms all night and know down to my bones that you're all right."

"Okay."

He set her on the gurney and stayed beside her as the paramedics covered her with a blanket and strapped her in. "You can say something besides *okay*, you know."

She curled her cold fingers into the front of his jacket. "I need you so much, Levi. I love you even more. With everything I have, everything I am. I will never *not* be there for you again. I love you."

He smiled, then leaned in and kissed her. "Okay."

* * * * *

Look for the next Protectors at K-9 Ranch story by USA TODAY *Bestselling Author Julie Miller, coming soon.*

Only from Harlequin Intrigue.